BABY-SITTERS LITTLE SISTER®

KAREN'S WORST DAY

DON'T MISS THE OTHER BABY-SITTERS LITTLE SISTER GRAPHIC NOVELS!

KAREN'S WITCH

KAREN'S ROLLER SKATES

ANN M. MARTIN
BABY-SITTERS LITTLE SISTER®

KAREN'S WORST DAY

A GRAPHIC NOVEL BY
KATY FARINA
WITH COLOR BY BRADEN LAMB

An Imprint of
SCHOLASTIC

This book is for
Read Marie Marcus,
Josh's little sister
A. M. M.

For Rian, my husband, who can turn my
worst days into my best days
K. F.

Text copyright © 2021 by Ann M. Martin
Art copyright © 2021 by Katy Farina

Library of Congress Control Number: 2019957367

ISBN 978-1-338-35619-9 (hardcover)
ISBN 978-1-338-35618-2 (paperback)

10 9 8 7 6 5 4 3 2 1   21 22 23 24 25

Printed in Malaysia   108
First edition, January 2021

Edited by Cassandra Pelham Fulton and David Levithan
Book design by Phil Falco and Shivana Sookdeo
Publisher: David Saylor

CHAPTER 1

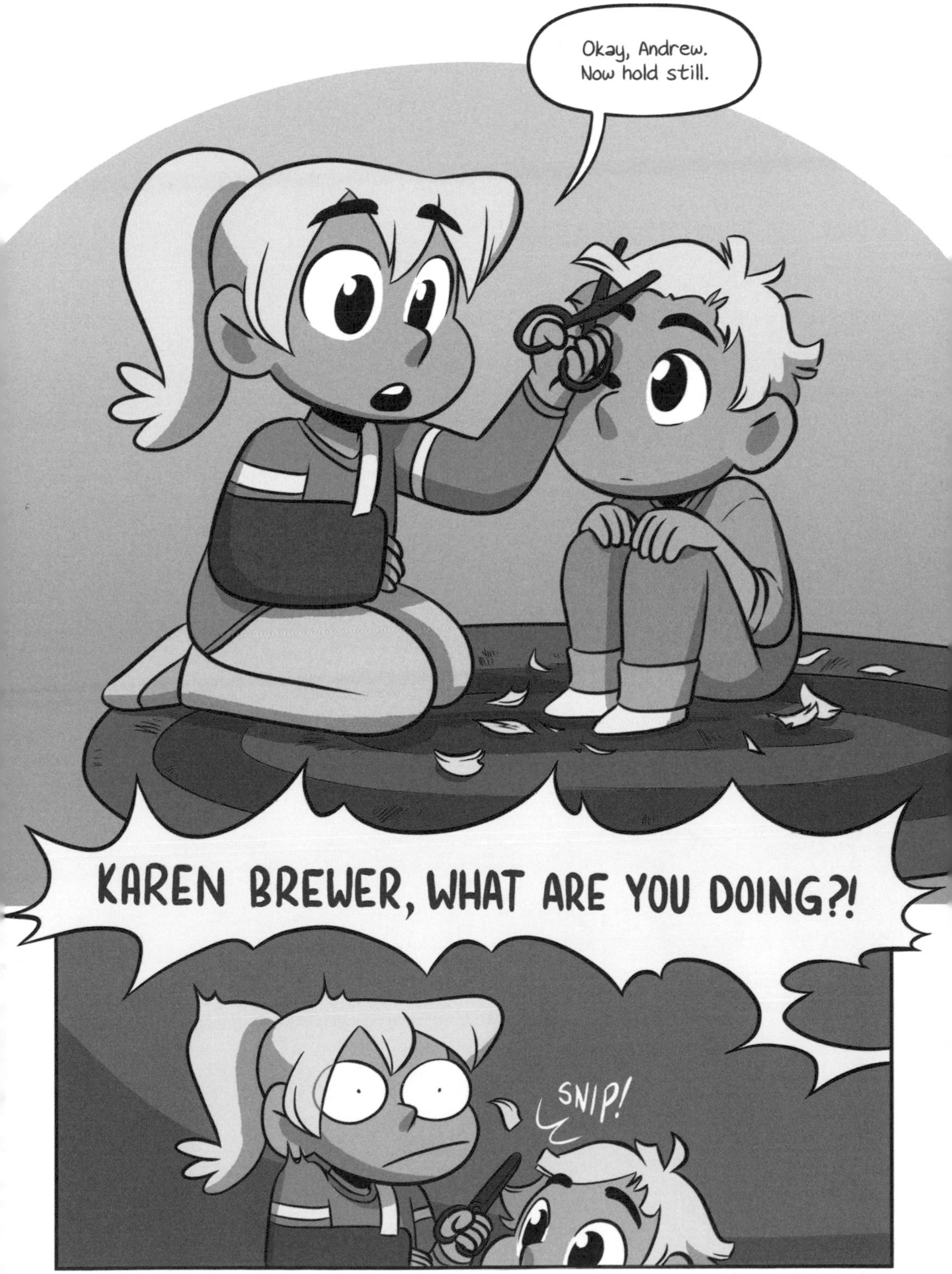

Okay, Andrew.
Now hold still.
KAREN BREWER, WHAT ARE YOU DOING?!
SNIP!

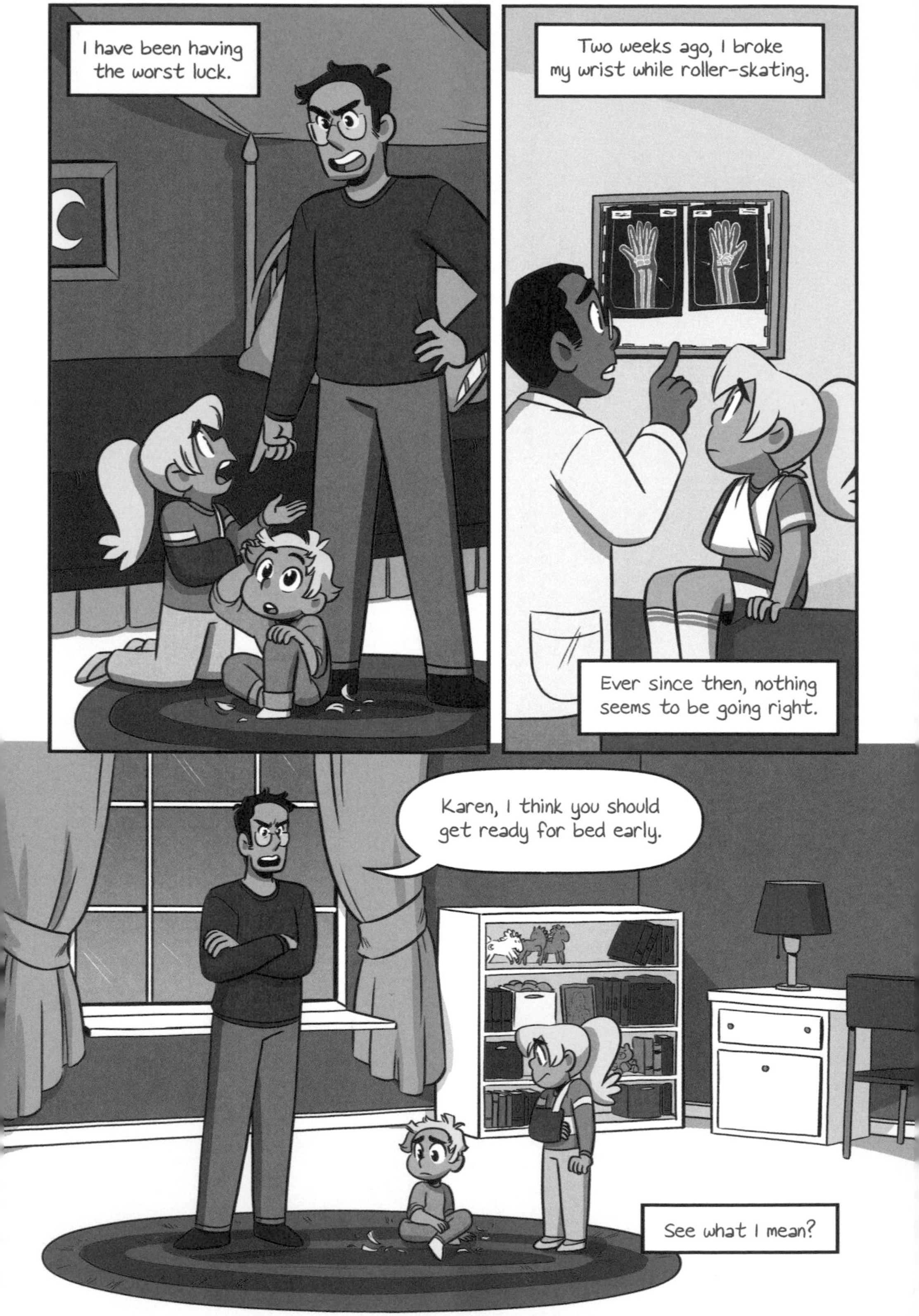
I have been having the worst luck.
Two weeks ago, I broke my wrist while roller-skating.
Ever since then, nothing seems to be going right.
Karen, I think you should get ready for bed early.
See what I mean?

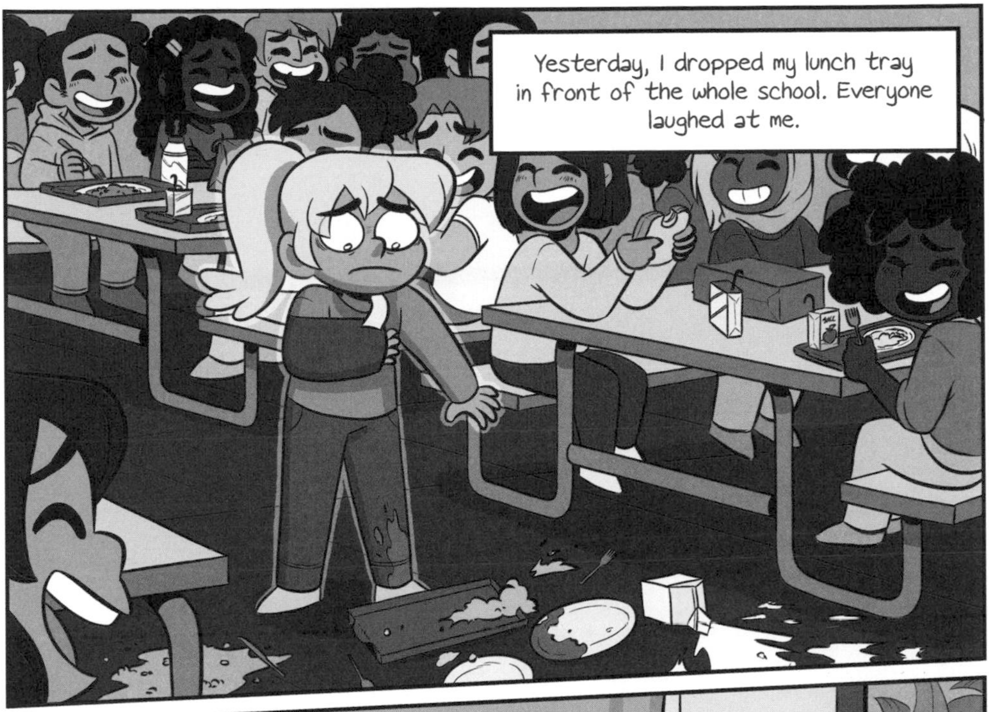
Yesterday, I dropped my lunch tray in front of the whole school. Everyone laughed at me.

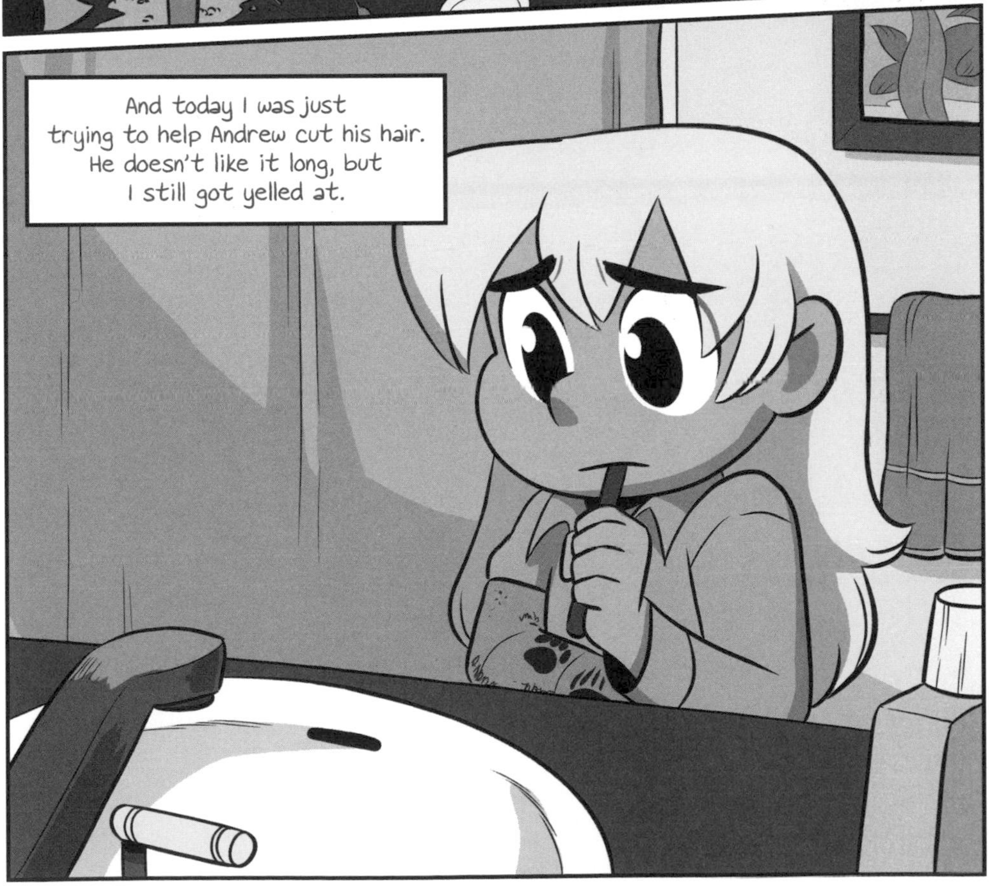
And today I was just trying to help Andrew cut his hair. He doesn't like it long, but I still got yelled at.

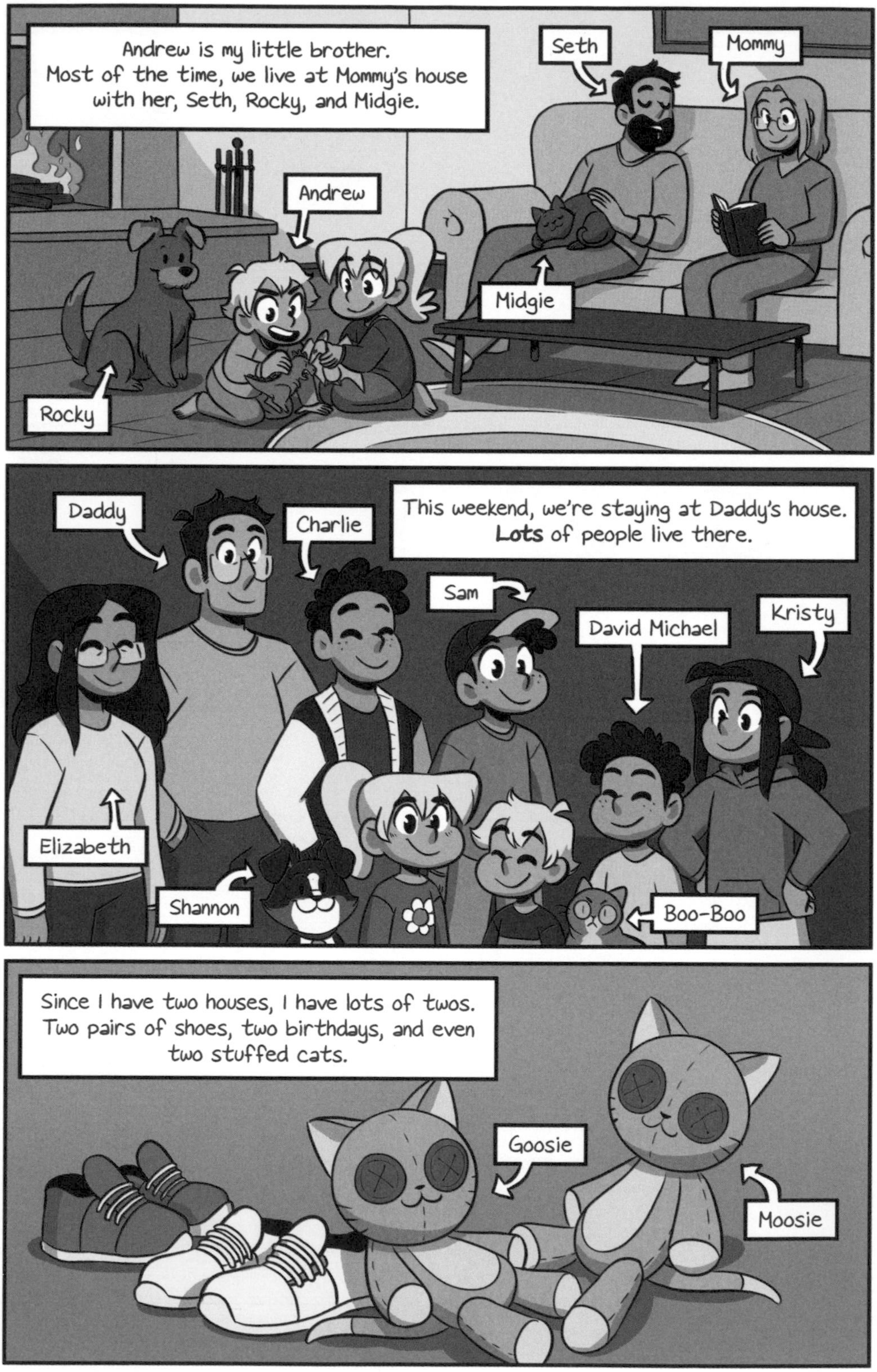
Andrew is my little brother.
Most of the time, we live at Mommy's house with her, Seth, Rocky, and Midgie.
Seth
Mommy
Andrew
Midgie
Rocky
Daddy
Charlie
This weekend, we're staying at Daddy's house. **Lots** of people live there.
Sam
David Michael
Kristy
Elizabeth
Shannon
Boo-Boo
Since I have two houses, I have lots of twos. Two pairs of shoes, two birthdays, and even two stuffed cats.
Goosie
Moosie

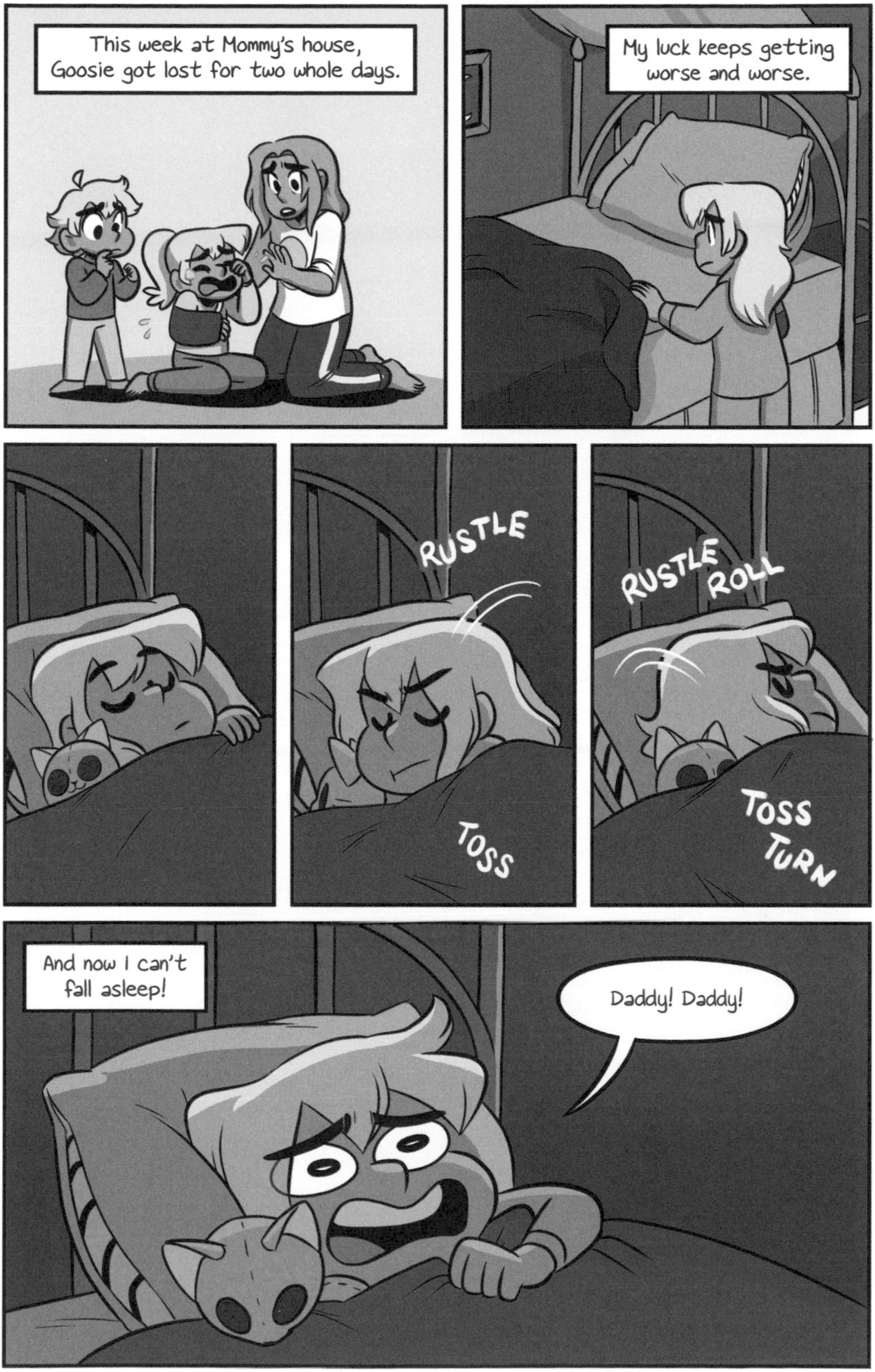
This week at Mommy's house, Goosie got lost for two whole days.
My luck keeps getting worse and worse.
RUSTLE
TOSS
RUSTLE ROLL
TOSS TURN
And now I can't fall asleep!
Daddy! Daddy!

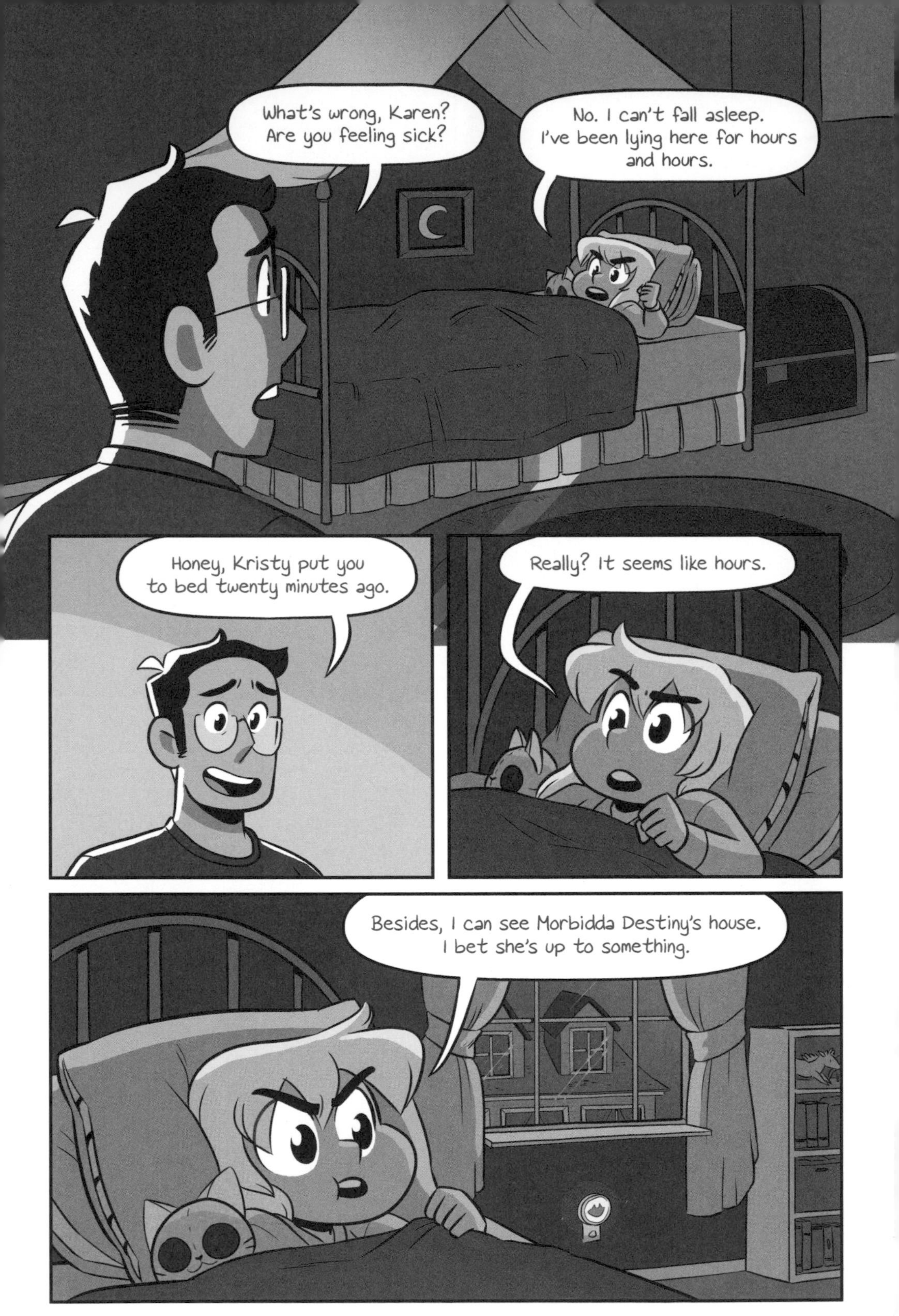
What's wrong, Karen?
Are you feeling sick?
No. I can't fall asleep.
I've been lying here for hours
and hours.
Honey, Kristy put you
to bed twenty minutes ago.
Really? It seems like hours.
Besides, I can see Morbidda Destiny's house.
I bet she's up to something.

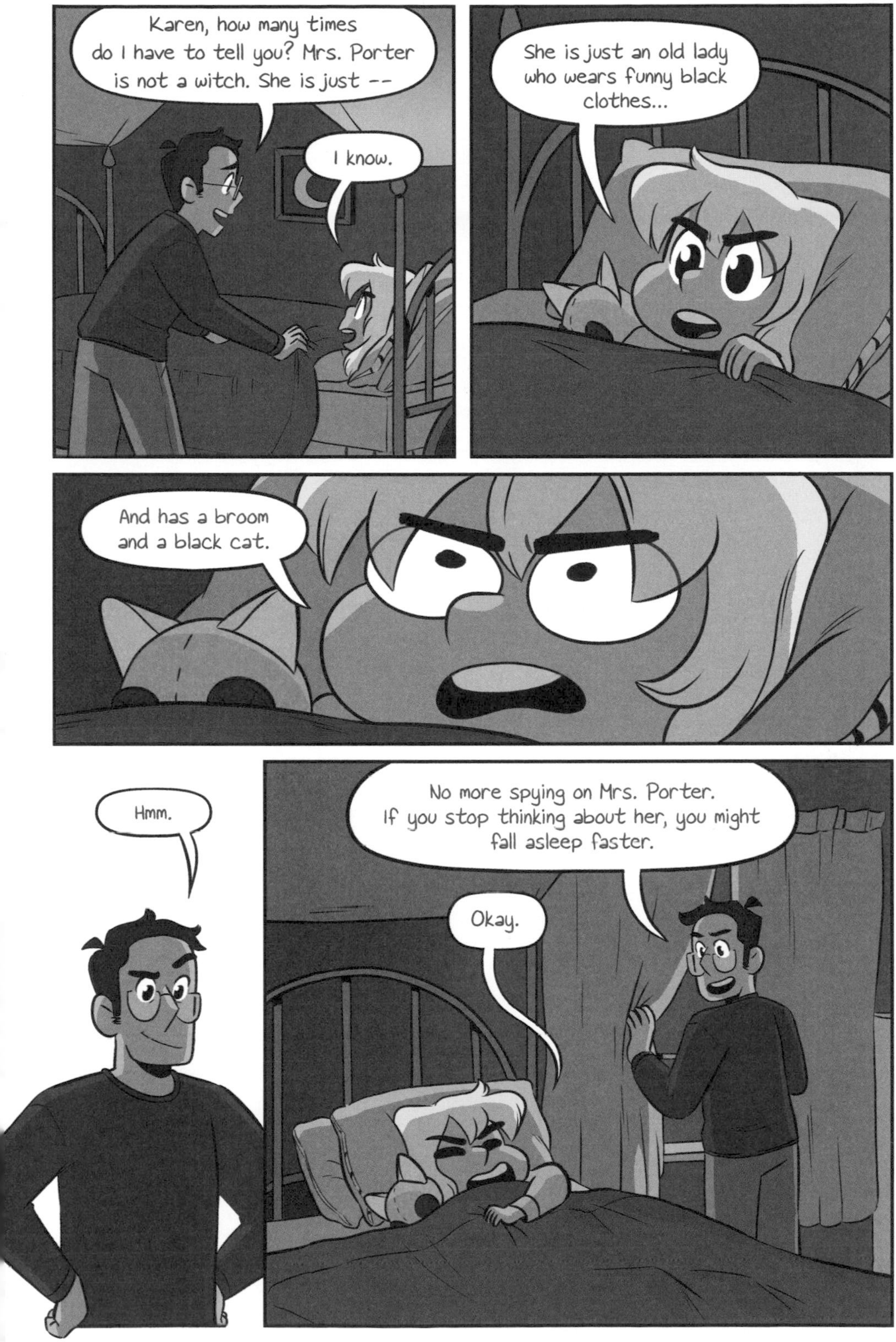
Karen, how many times do I have to tell you? Mrs. Porter is not a witch. She is just --
I know.
She is just an old lady who wears funny black clothes...
And has a broom and a black cat.
Hmm.
No more spying on Mrs. Porter. If you stop thinking about her, you might fall asleep faster.
Okay.

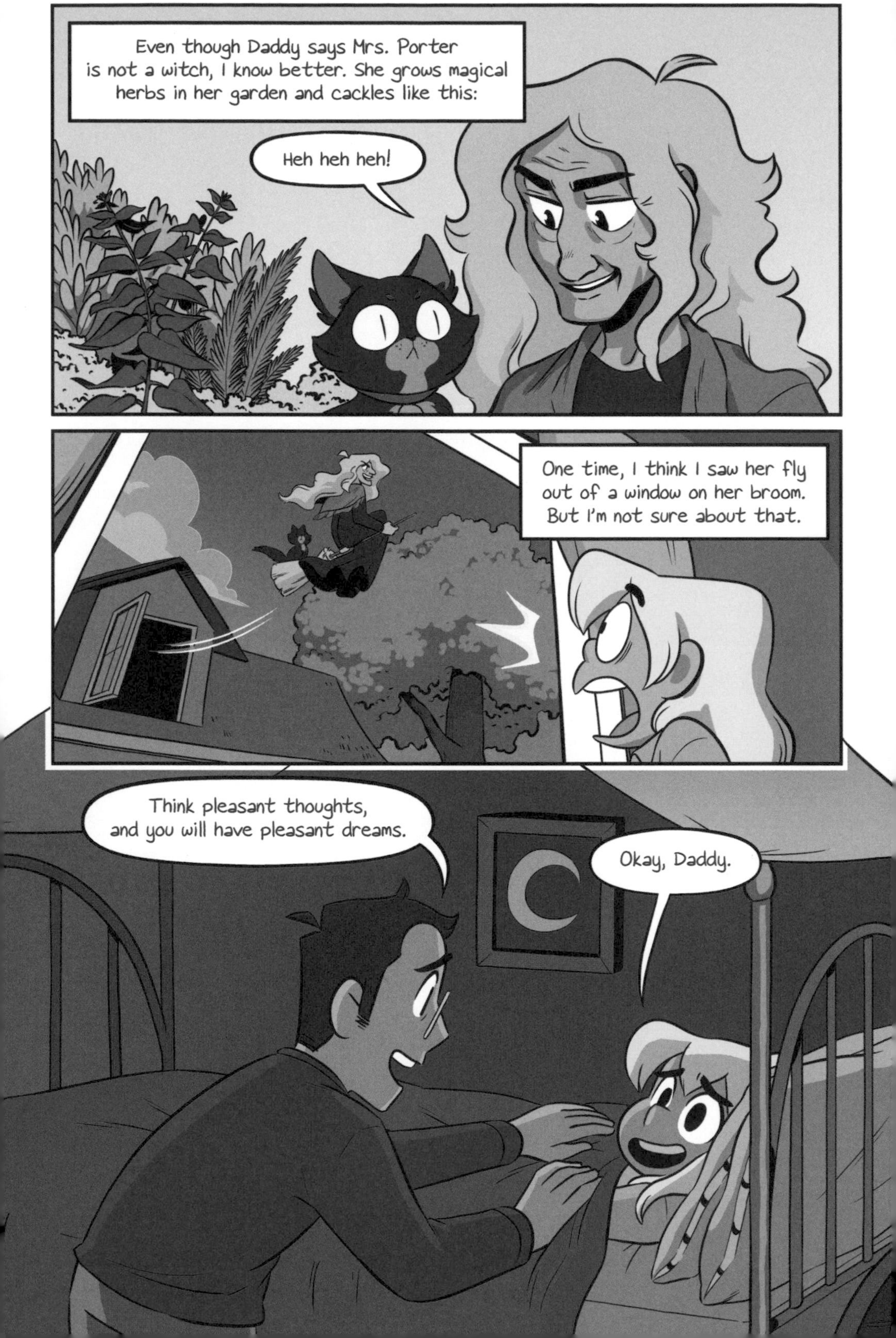
Even though Daddy says Mrs. Porter is not a witch, I know better. She grows magical herbs in her garden and cackles like this:
Heh heh heh!
One time, I think I saw her fly out of a window on her broom. But I'm not sure about that.
Think pleasant thoughts, and you will have pleasant dreams.
Okay, Daddy.

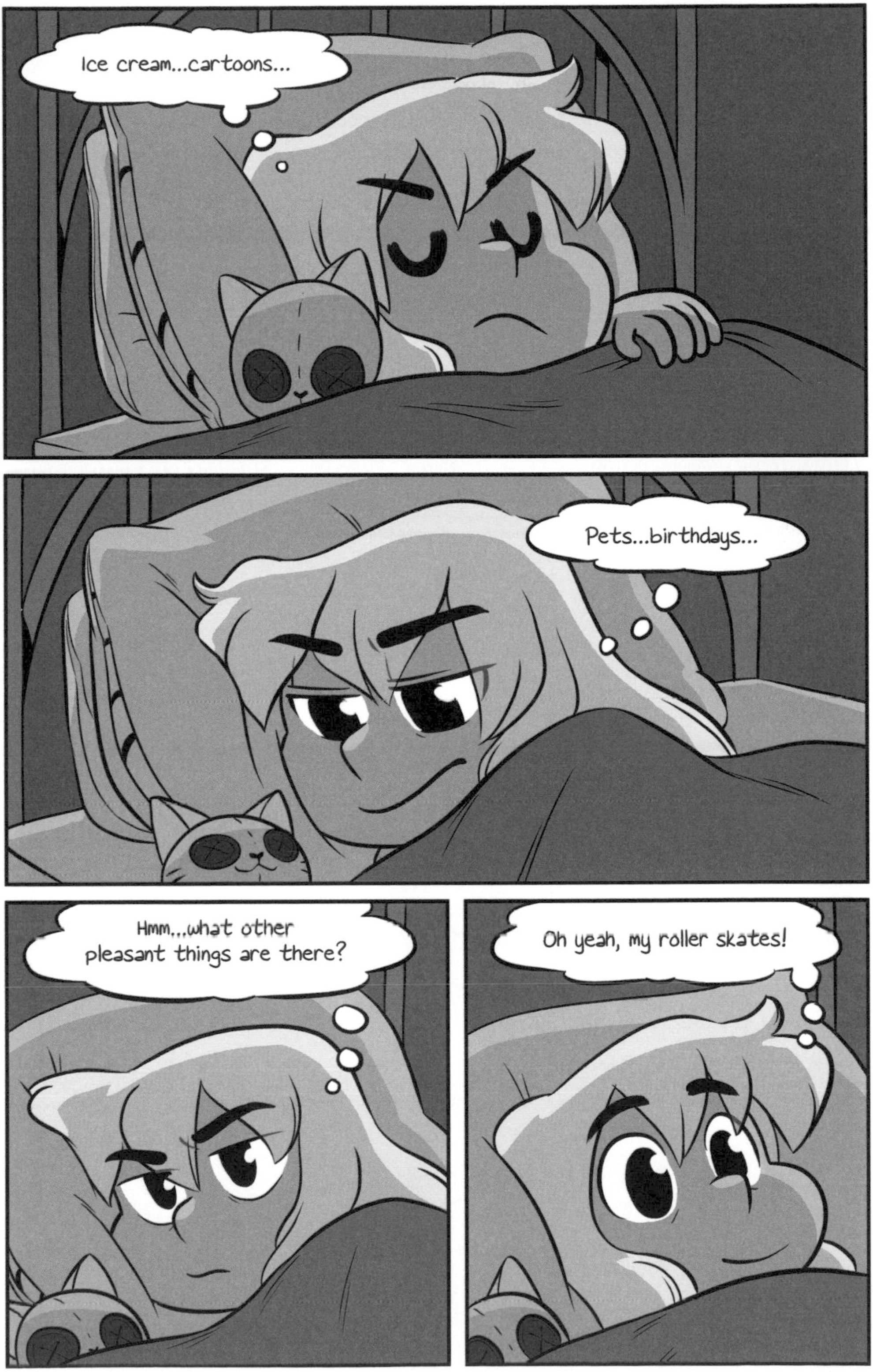
Ice cream...cartoons...
Pets...birthdays...
Hmm...what other pleasant things are there?
Oh yeah, my roller skates!

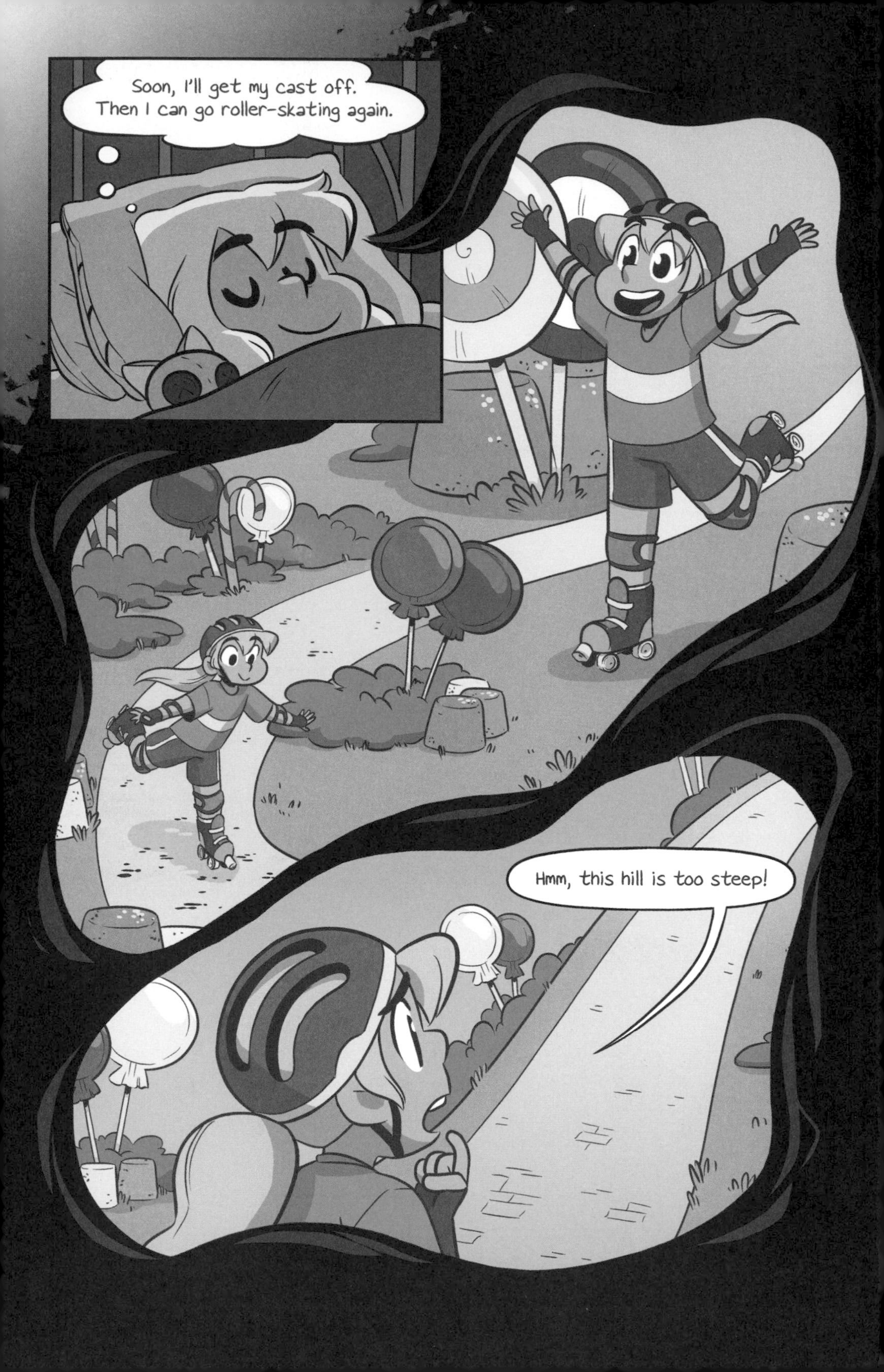
Soon, I'll get my cast off.
Then I can go roller-skating again.
Hmm, this hill is too steep!

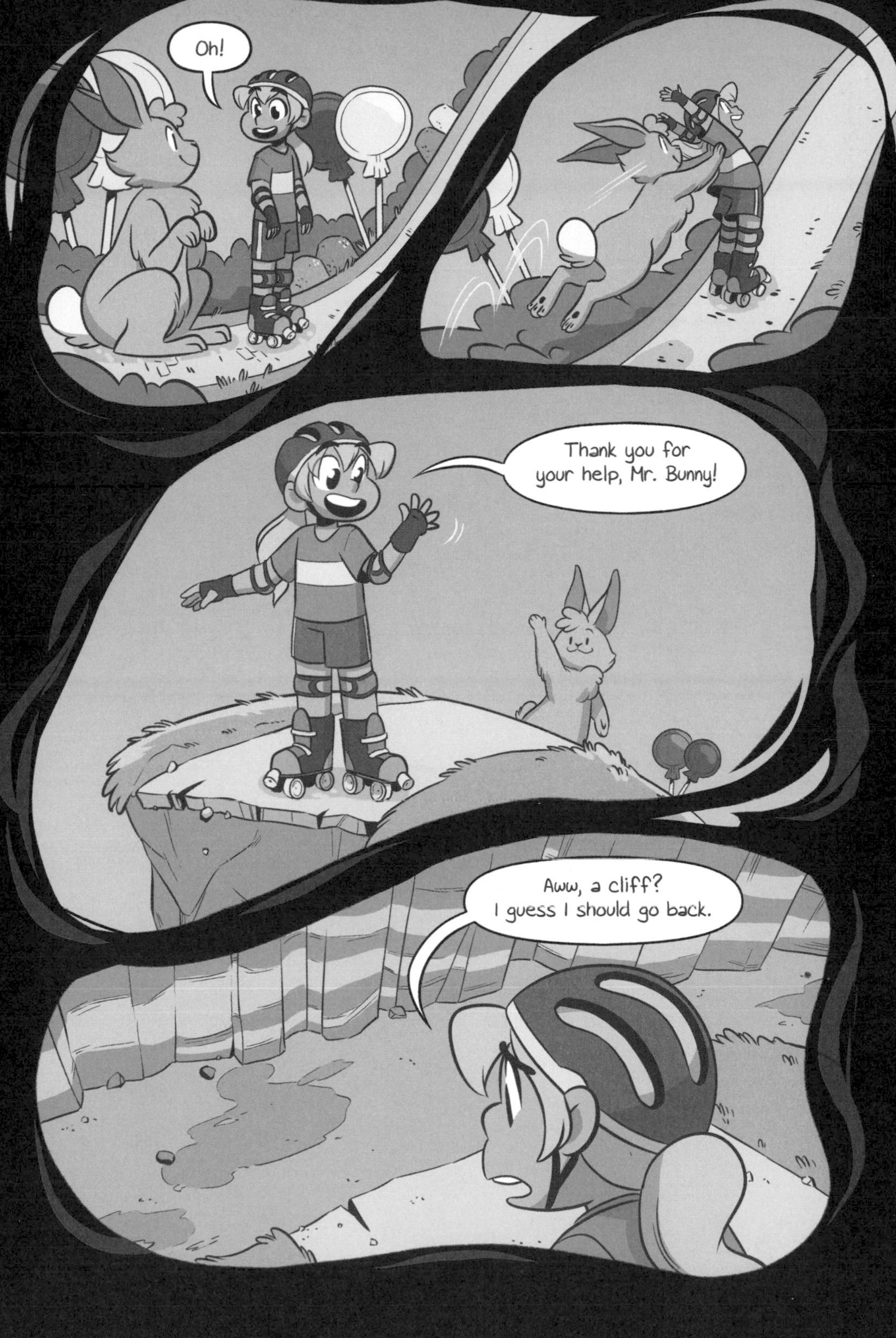
Oh!
Thank you for your help, Mr. Bunny!
Aww, a cliff? I guess I should go back.

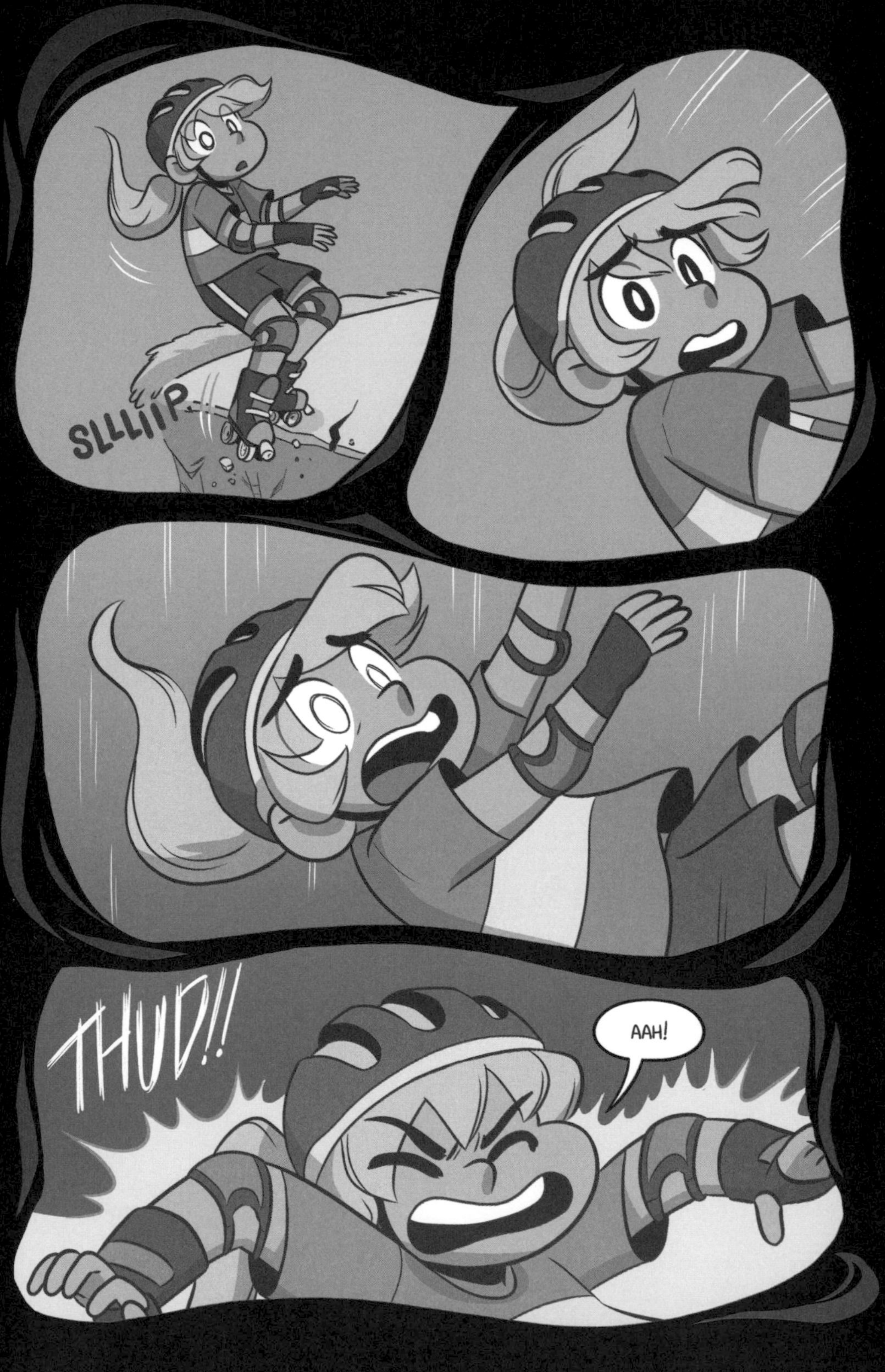
SLLLIIP
THUD!!
AAH!

CHAPTER 2

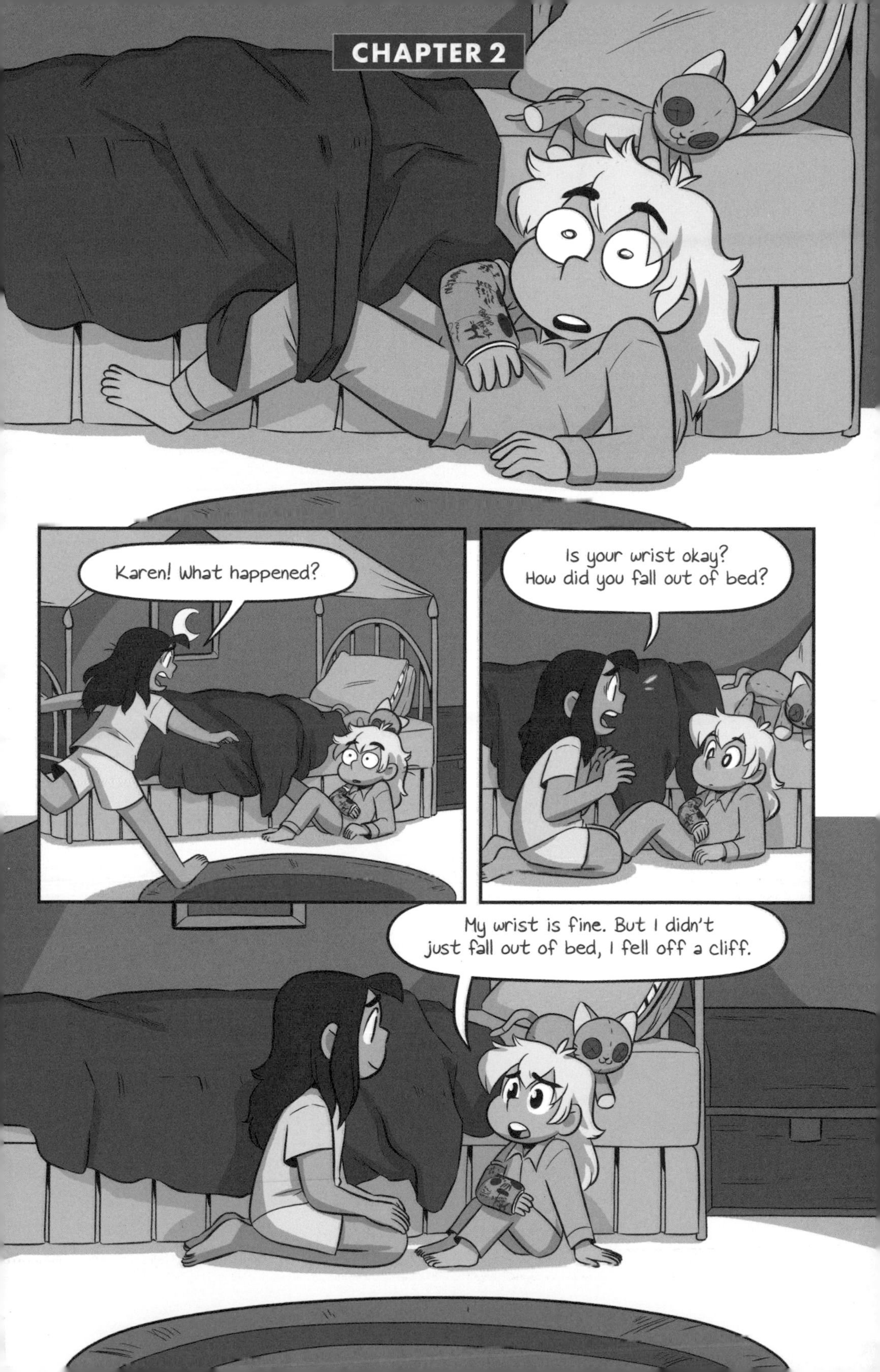
Karen! What happened?
Is your wrist okay?
How did you fall out of bed?
My wrist is fine. But I didn't
just fall out of bed, I fell off a cliff.

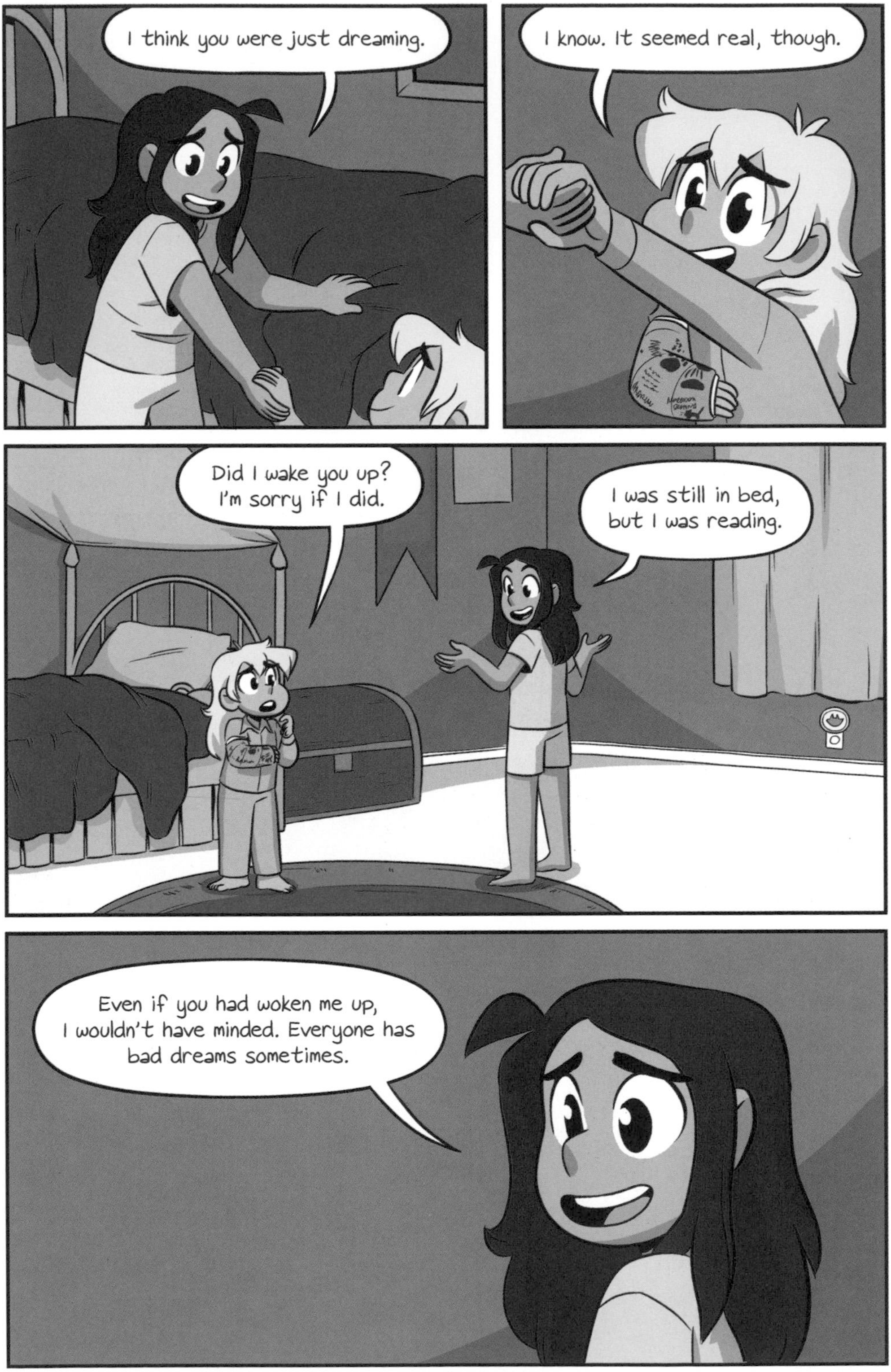
I think you were just dreaming.
I know. It seemed real, though.
Did I wake you up? I'm sorry if I did.
I was still in bed, but I was reading.
Even if you had woken me up, I wouldn't have minded. Everyone has bad dreams sometimes.

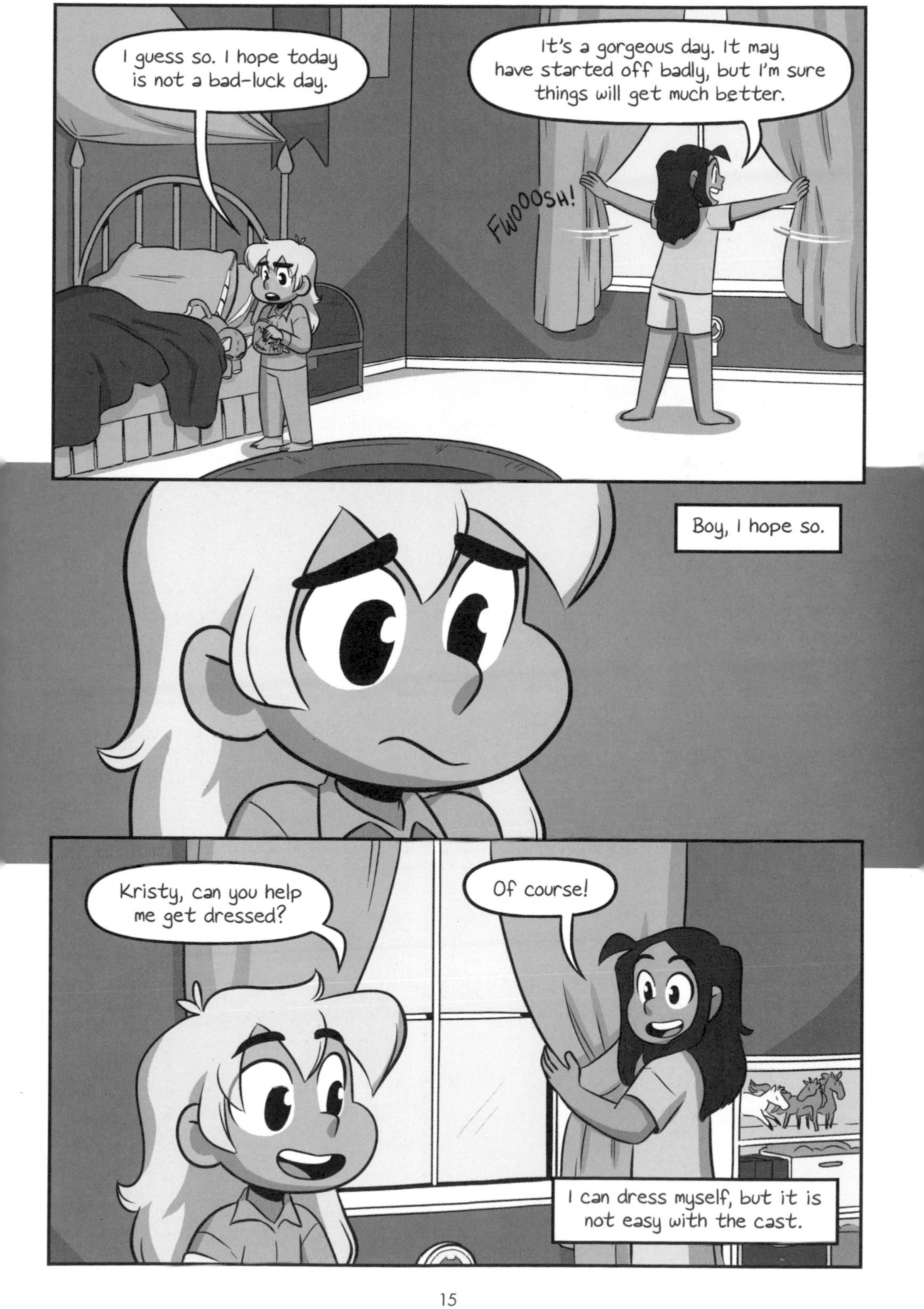
I guess so. I hope today is not a bad-luck day.
It's a gorgeous day. It may have started off badly, but I'm sure things will get much better.
FWOOOSH!
Boy, I hope so.
Kristy, can you help me get dressed?
Of course!
I can dress myself, but it is not easy with the cast.

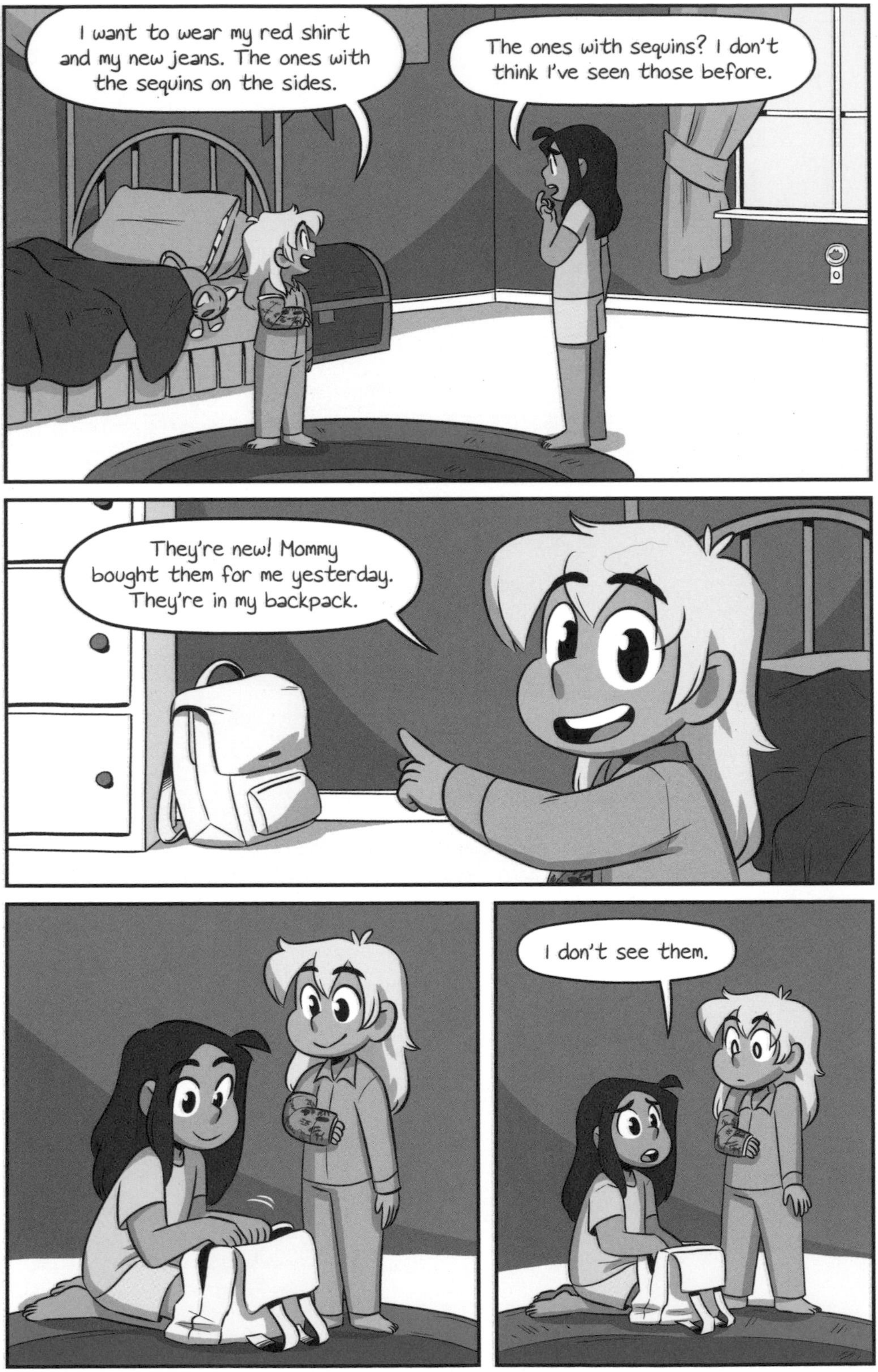
I want to wear my red shirt and my new jeans. The ones with the sequins on the sides.
The ones with sequins? I don't think I've seen those before.
They're new! Mommy bought them for me yesterday. They're in my backpack.
I don't see them.

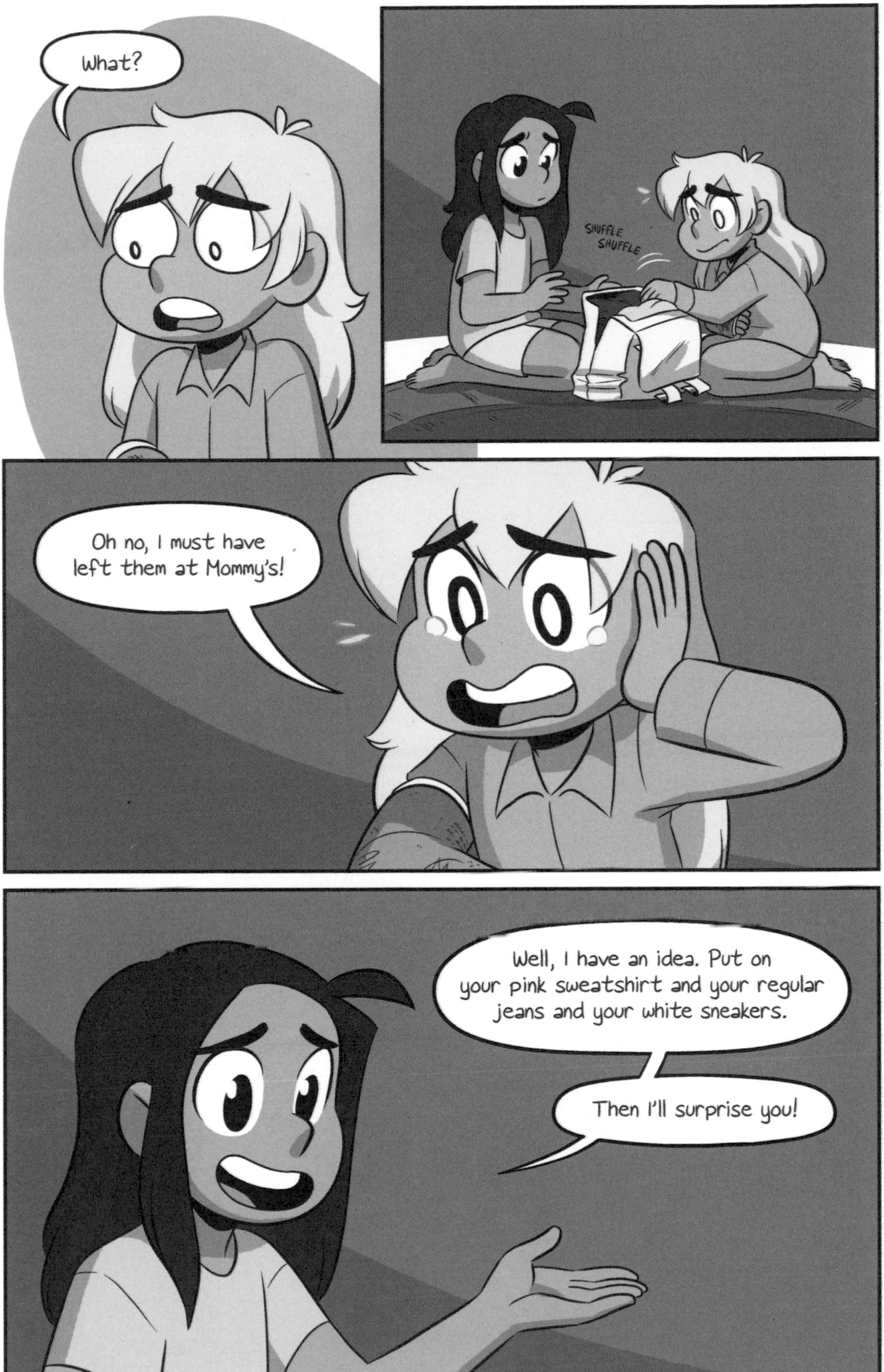
What?
SHUFFLE SHUFFLE
Oh no, I must have left them at Mommy's!
Well, I have an idea. Put on your pink sweatshirt and your regular jeans and your white sneakers.
Then I'll surprise you!

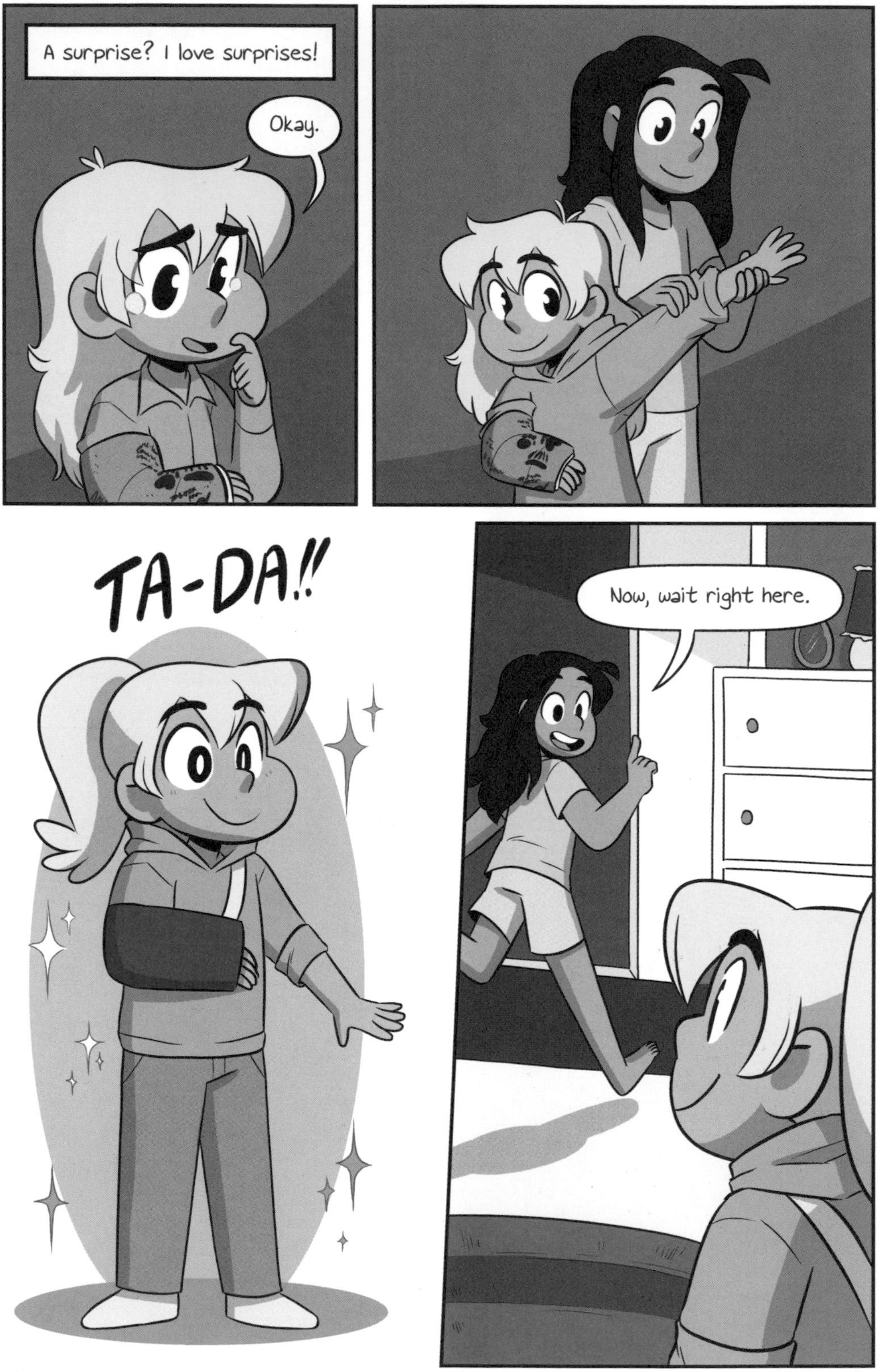
A surprise? I love surprises!
Okay.
TA-DA!!
Now, wait right here.

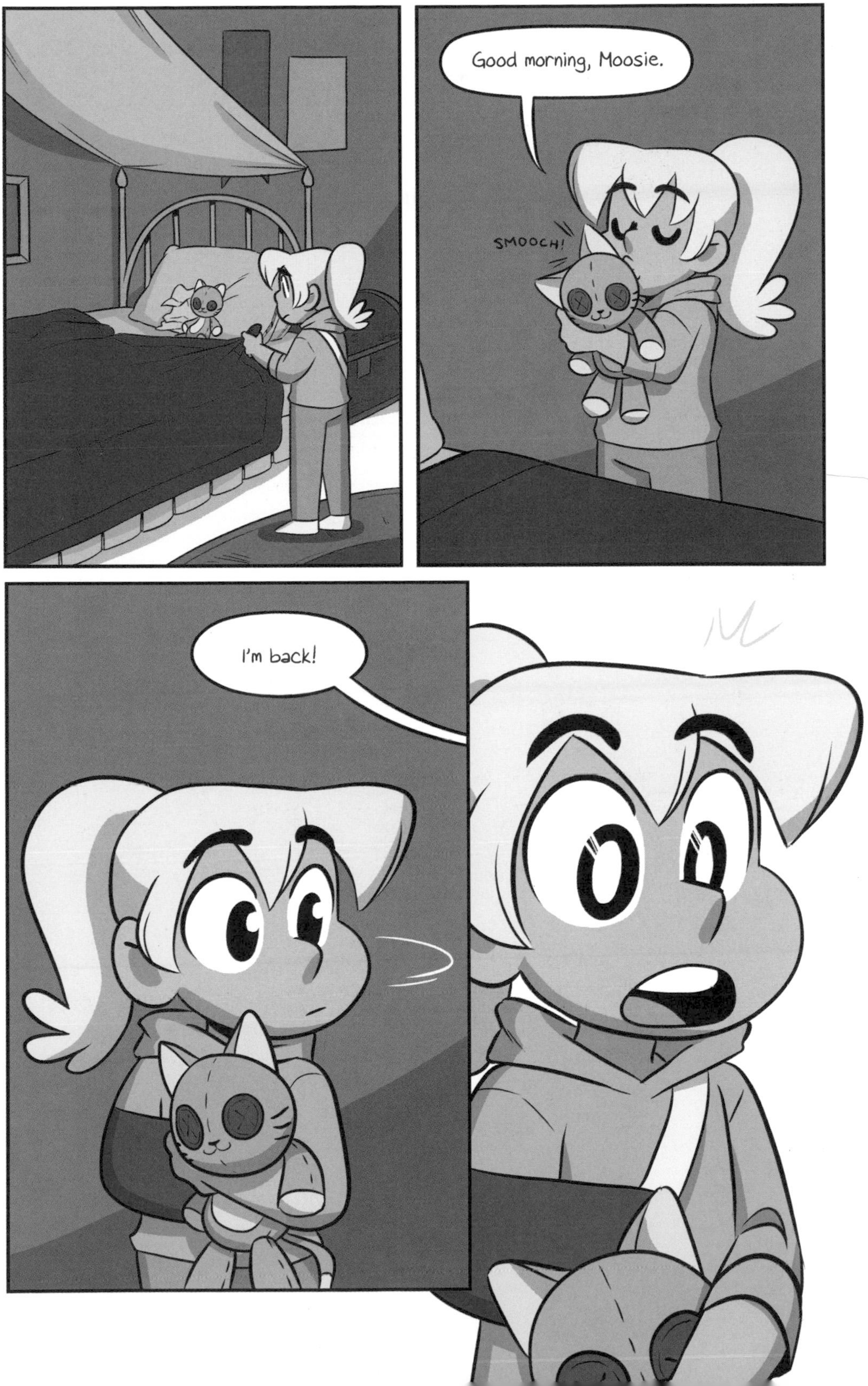
Good morning, Moosie.
SMOOCH!
I'm back!

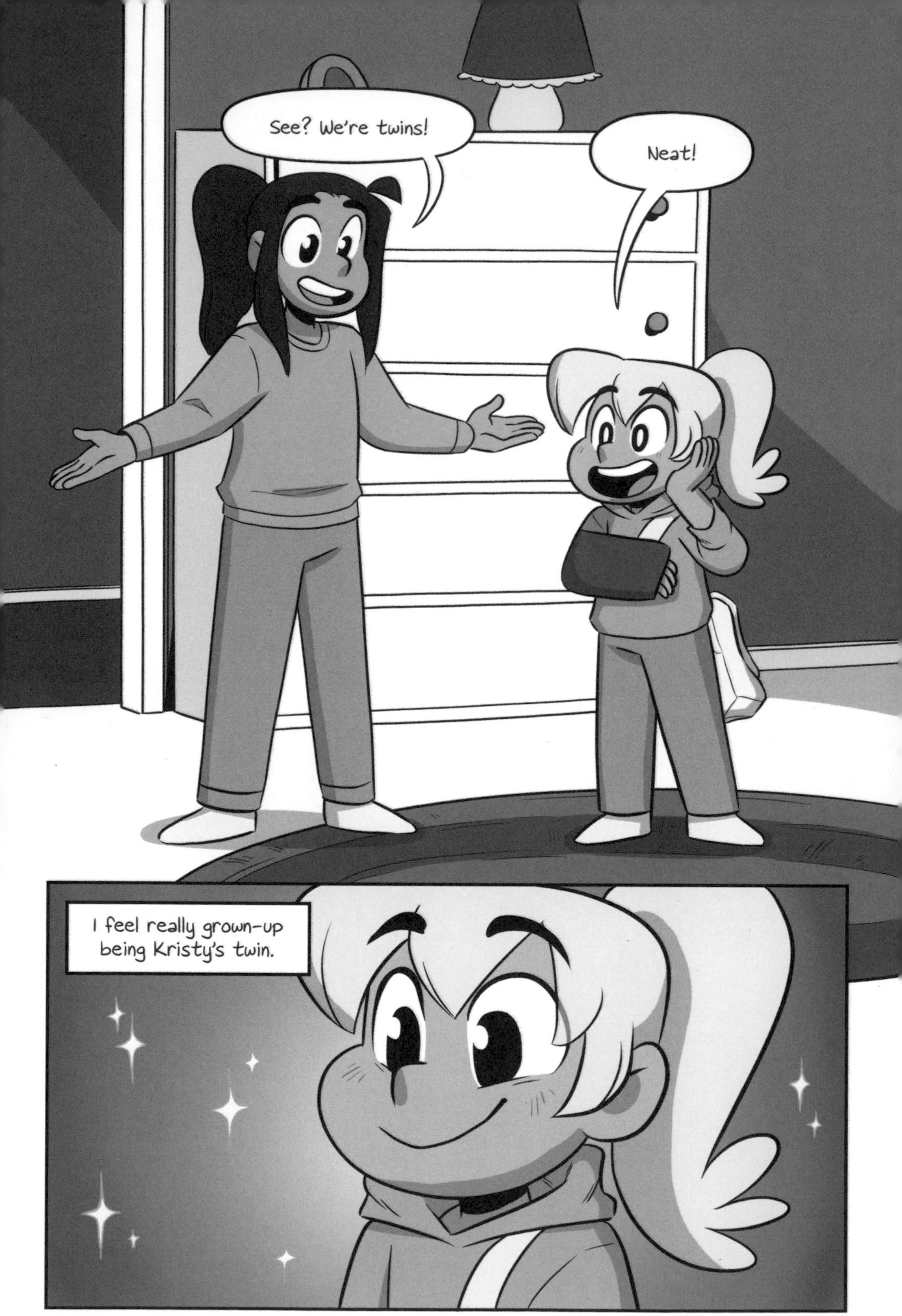
See? We're twins!
Neat!
I feel really grown-up being Kristy's twin.

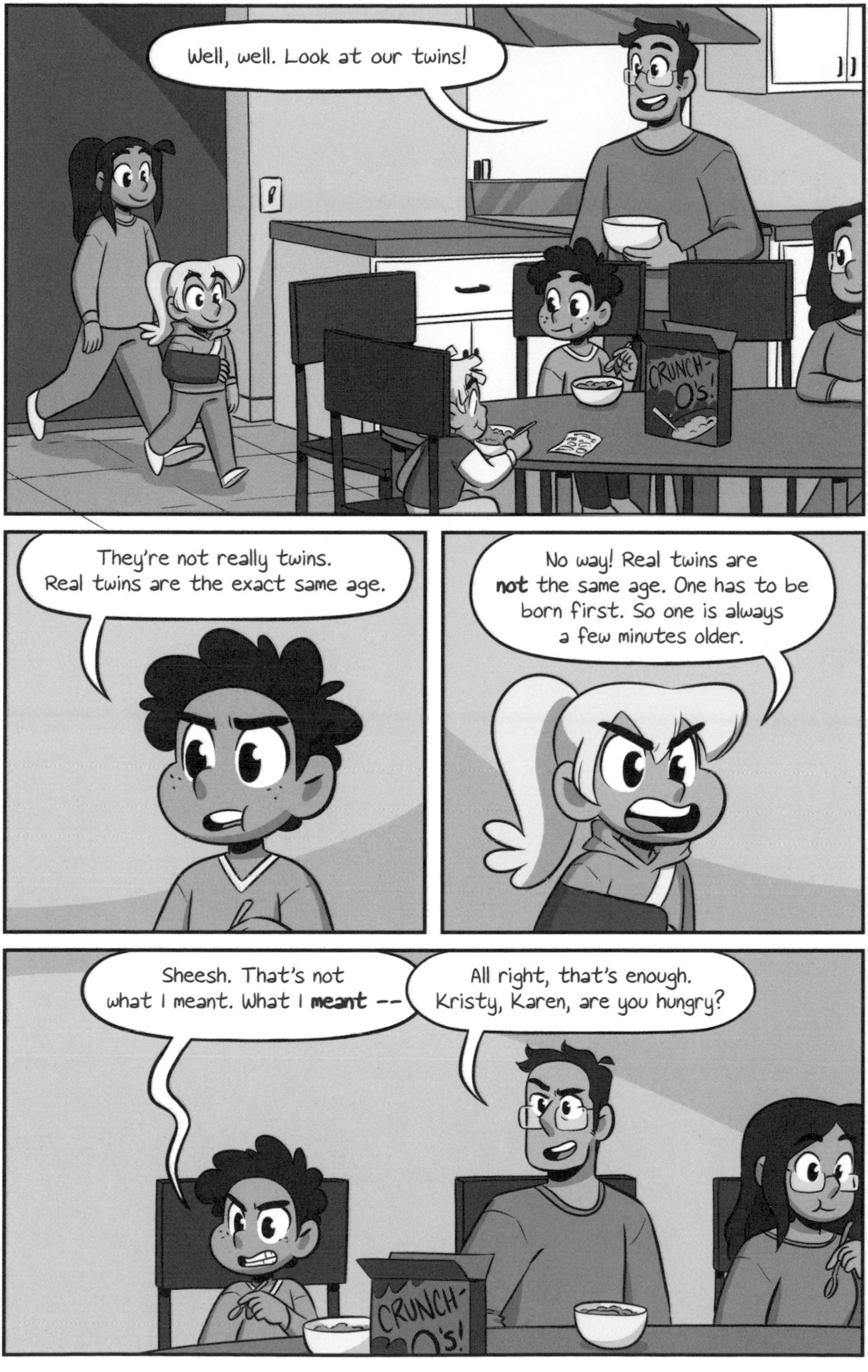
Well, well. Look at our twins!
CRUNCH-O's!
They're not really twins. Real twins are the exact same age.
No way! Real twins are **not** the same age. One has to be born first. So one is always a few minutes older.
Sheesh. That's not what I meant. What I **meant** --
All right, that's enough. Kristy, Karen, are you hungry?
CRUNCH-O's!

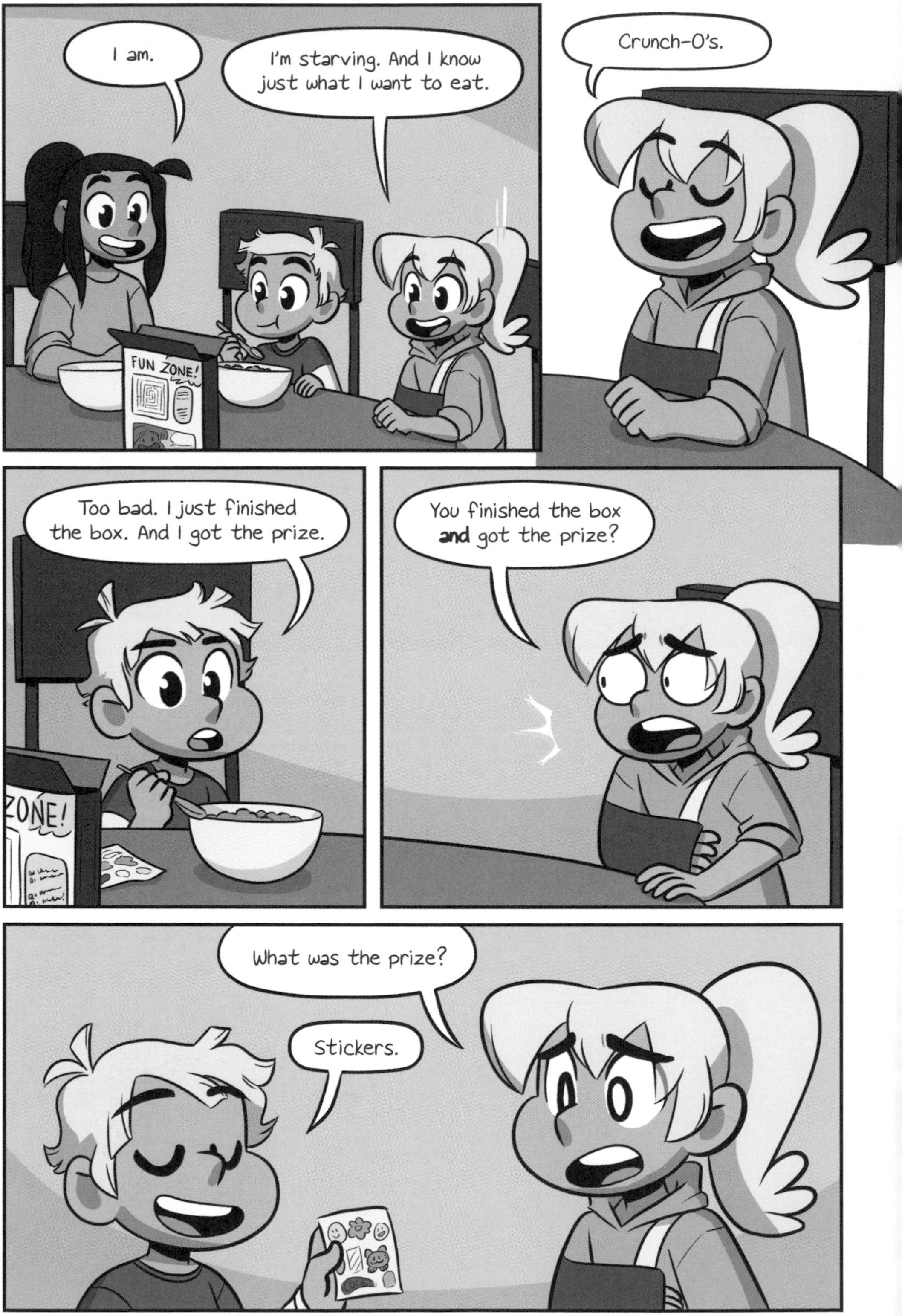
I am.
I'm starving. And I know just what I want to eat.
Crunch-O's.
FUN ZONE!
Too bad. I just finished the box. And I got the prize.
ZONE!
You finished the box **and** got the prize?
What was the prize?
Stickers.

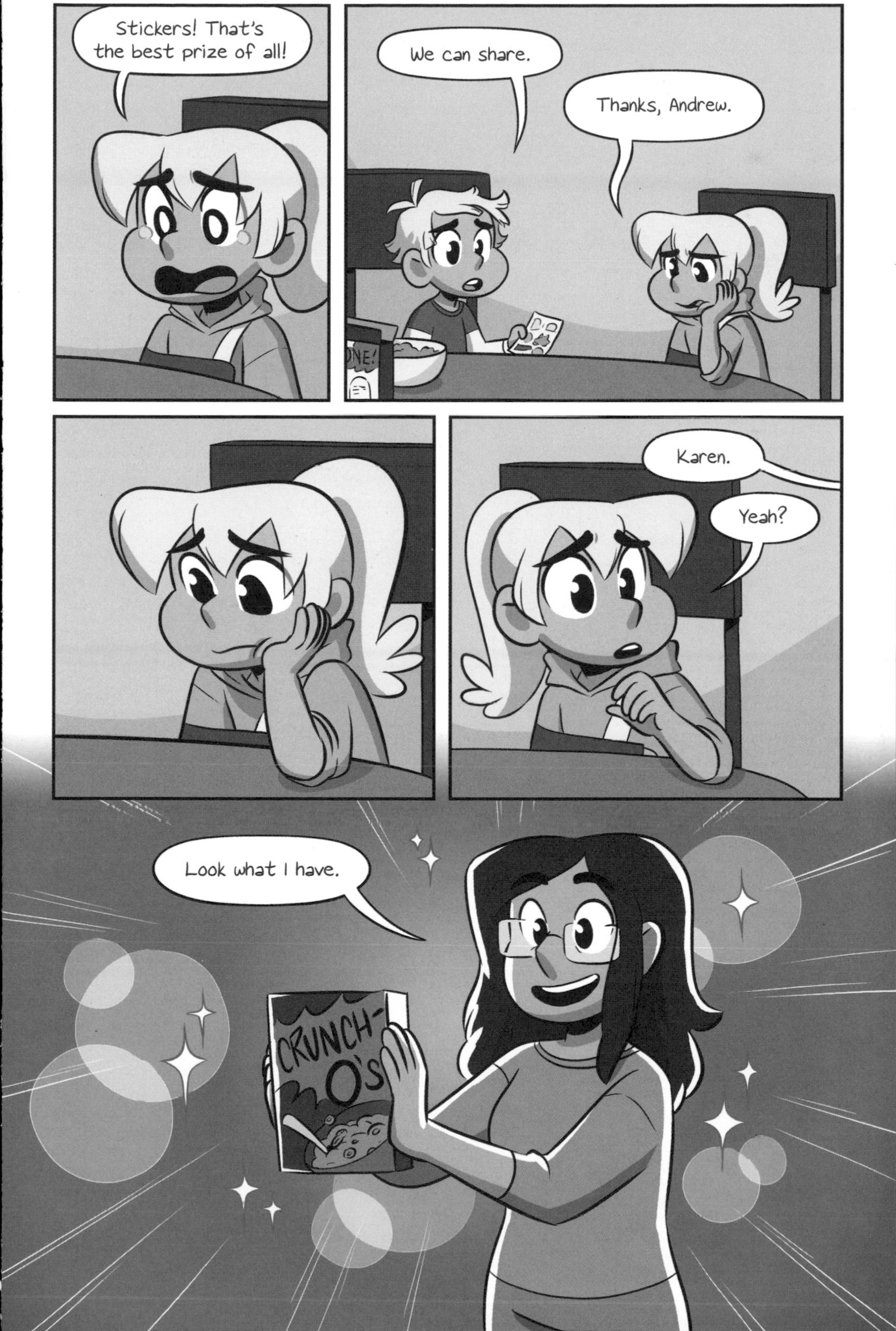
Stickers! That's the best prize of all!
We can share.
Thanks, Andrew.
Karen.
Yeah?
Look what I have.
CRUNCH-O's

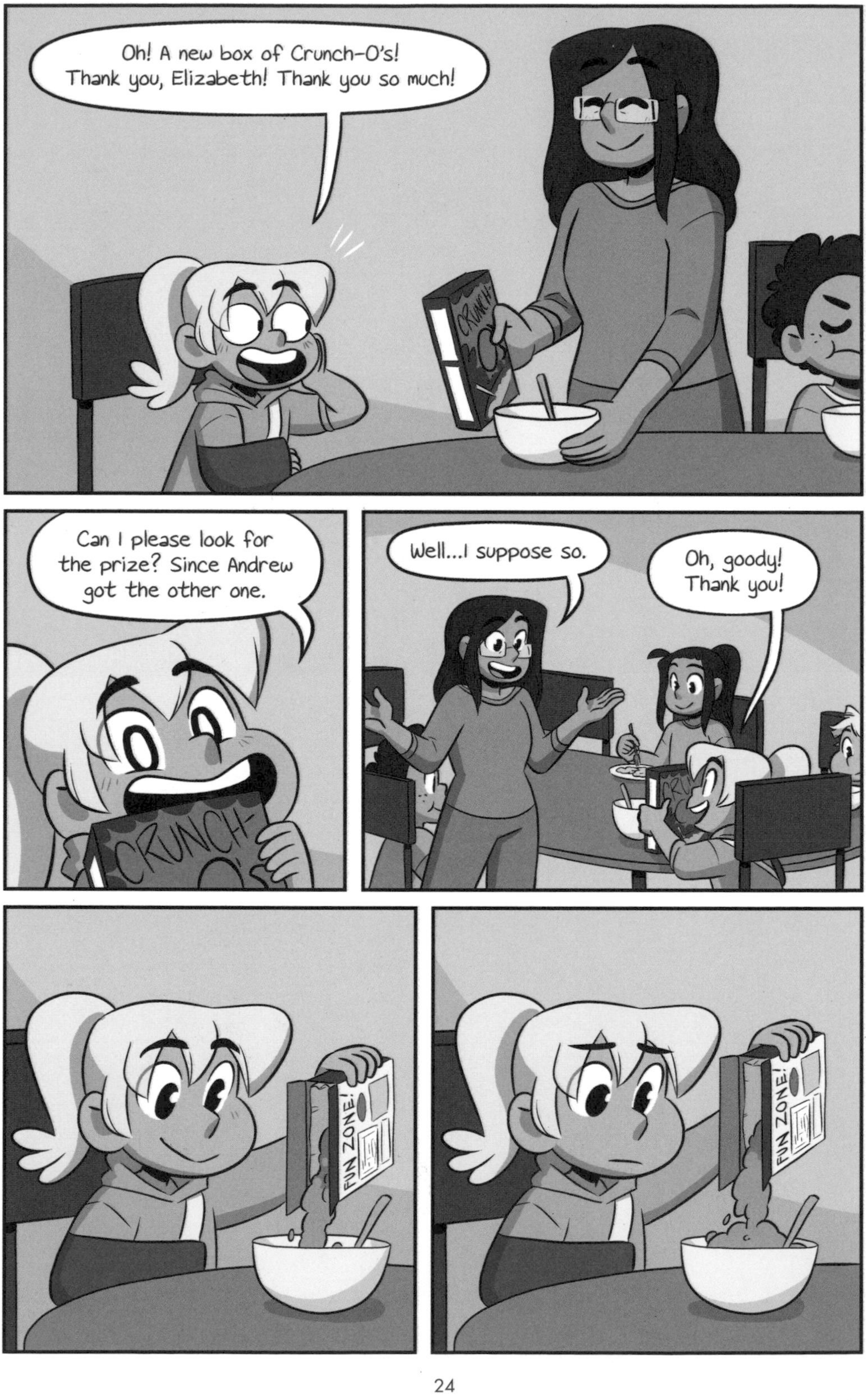
Oh! A new box of Crunch-O's! Thank you, Elizabeth! Thank you so much!
CRUNCH-
Can I please look for the prize? Since Andrew got the other one.
CRUNCH-O'S
Well...I suppose so.
Oh, goody! Thank you!
FUN ZONE!
FUN ZONE!

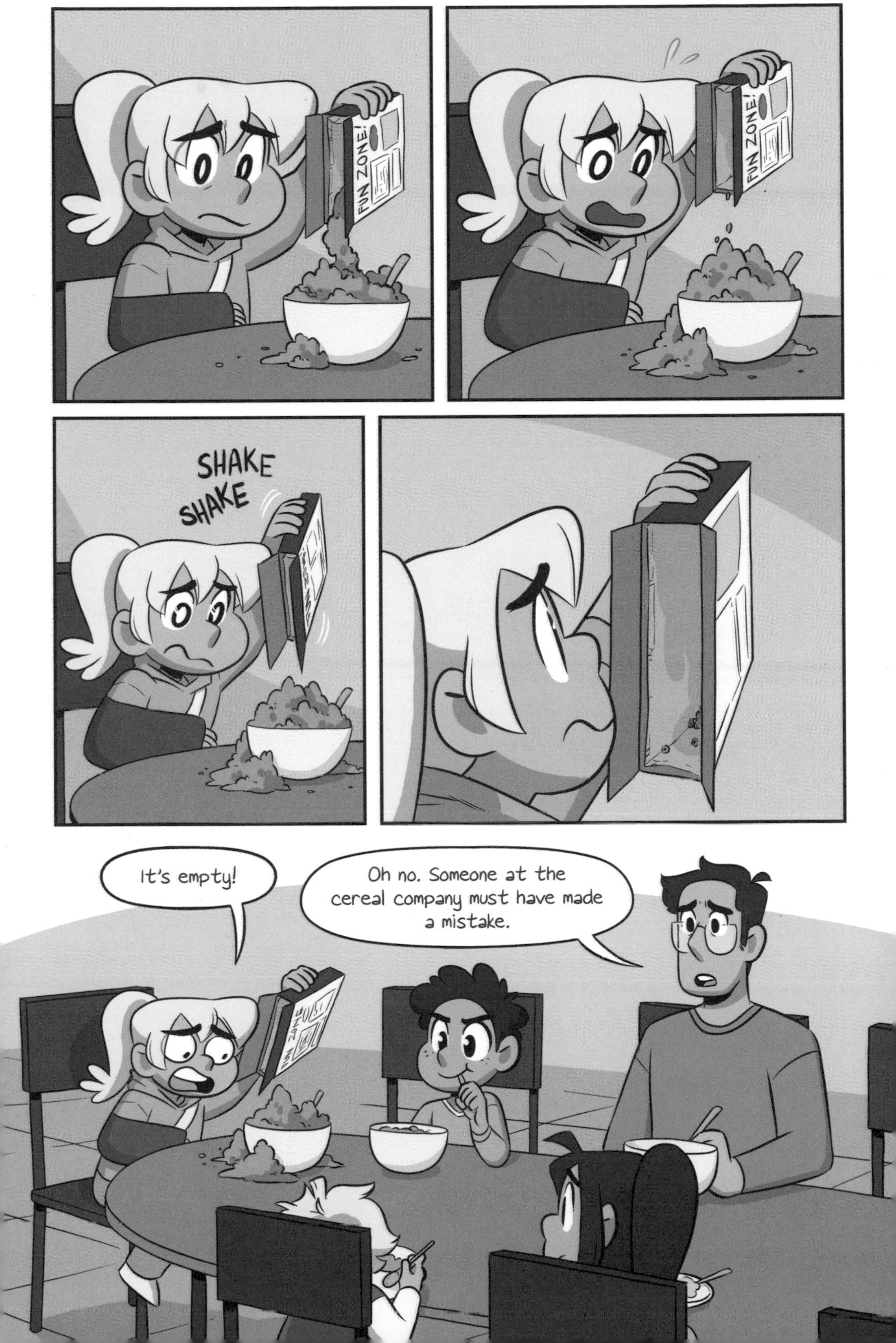
FUN ZONE!
FUN ZONE!
SHAKE
SHAKE
It's empty!
Oh no. Someone at the cereal company must have made a mistake.

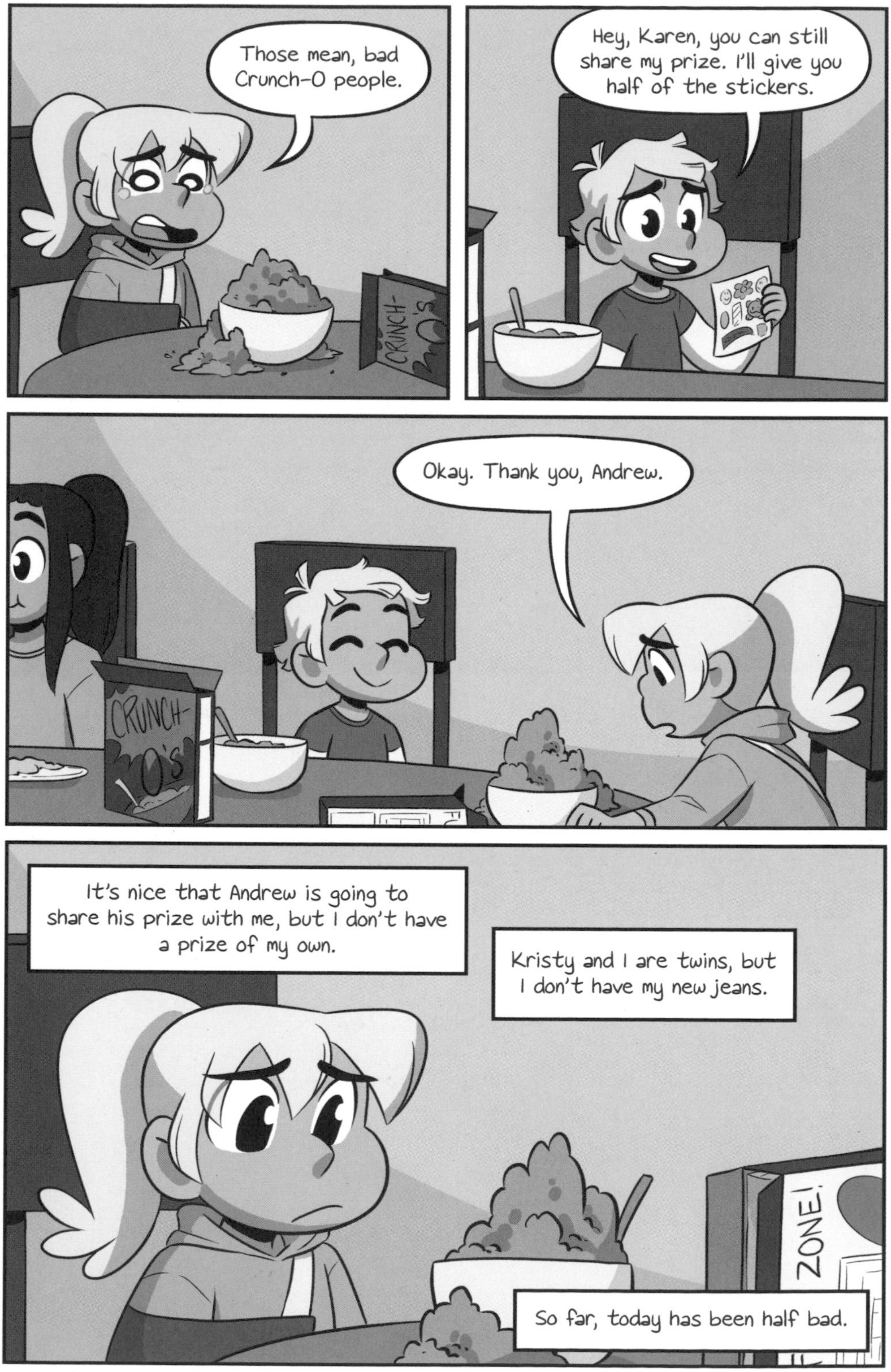

Those mean, bad Crunch-O people.
CRUNCH-O's
Hey, Karen, you can still share my prize. I'll give you half of the stickers.
Okay. Thank you, Andrew.
CRUNCH-O's
It's nice that Andrew is going to share his prize with me, but I don't have a prize of my own.
Kristy and I are twins, but I don't have my new jeans.
ZONE!
So far, today has been half bad.

CHAPTER 3

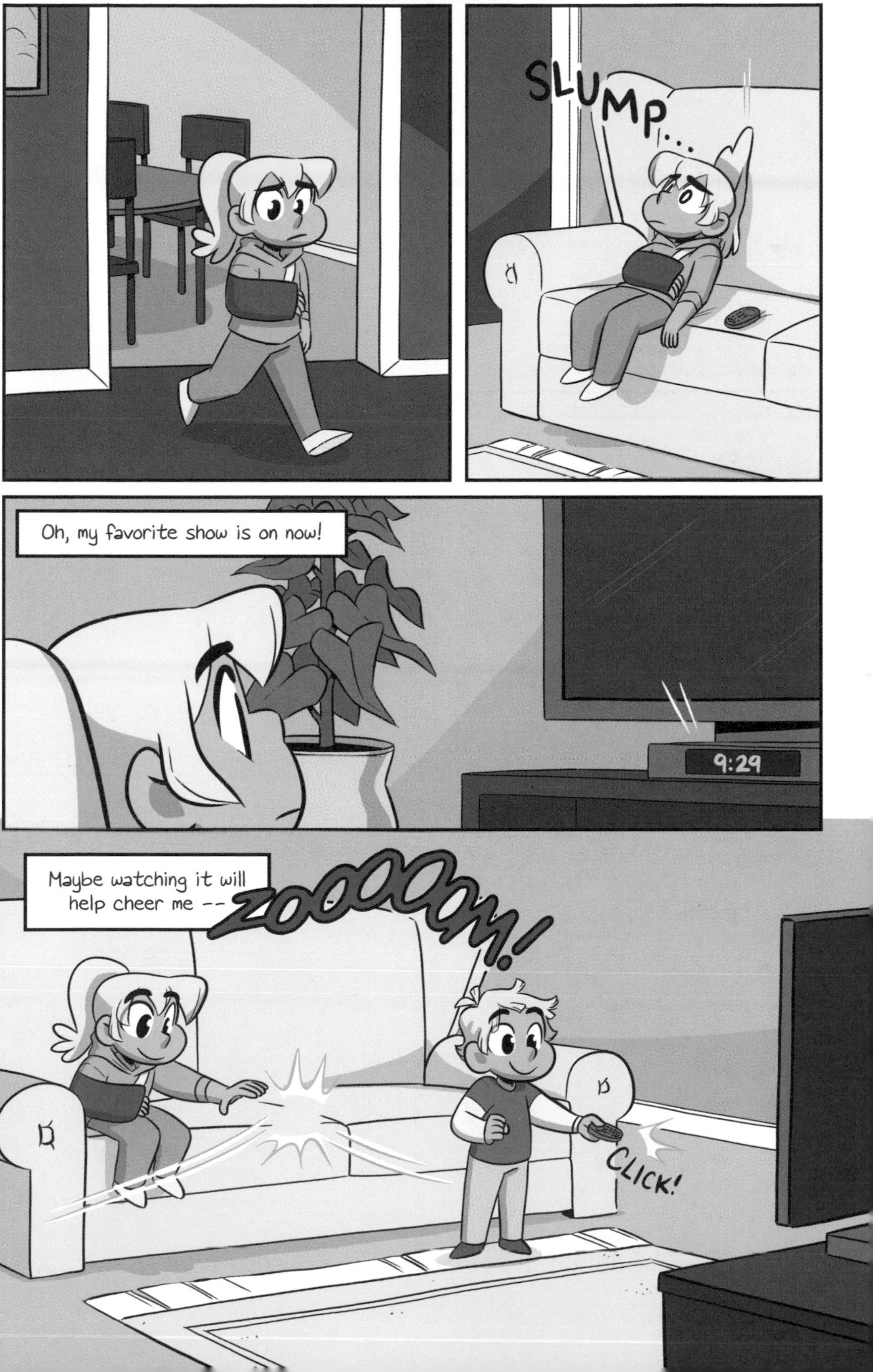
SLUMP...
Oh, my favorite show is on now!
9:29
Maybe watching it will help cheer me --
ZOOOOOM!
CLICK!

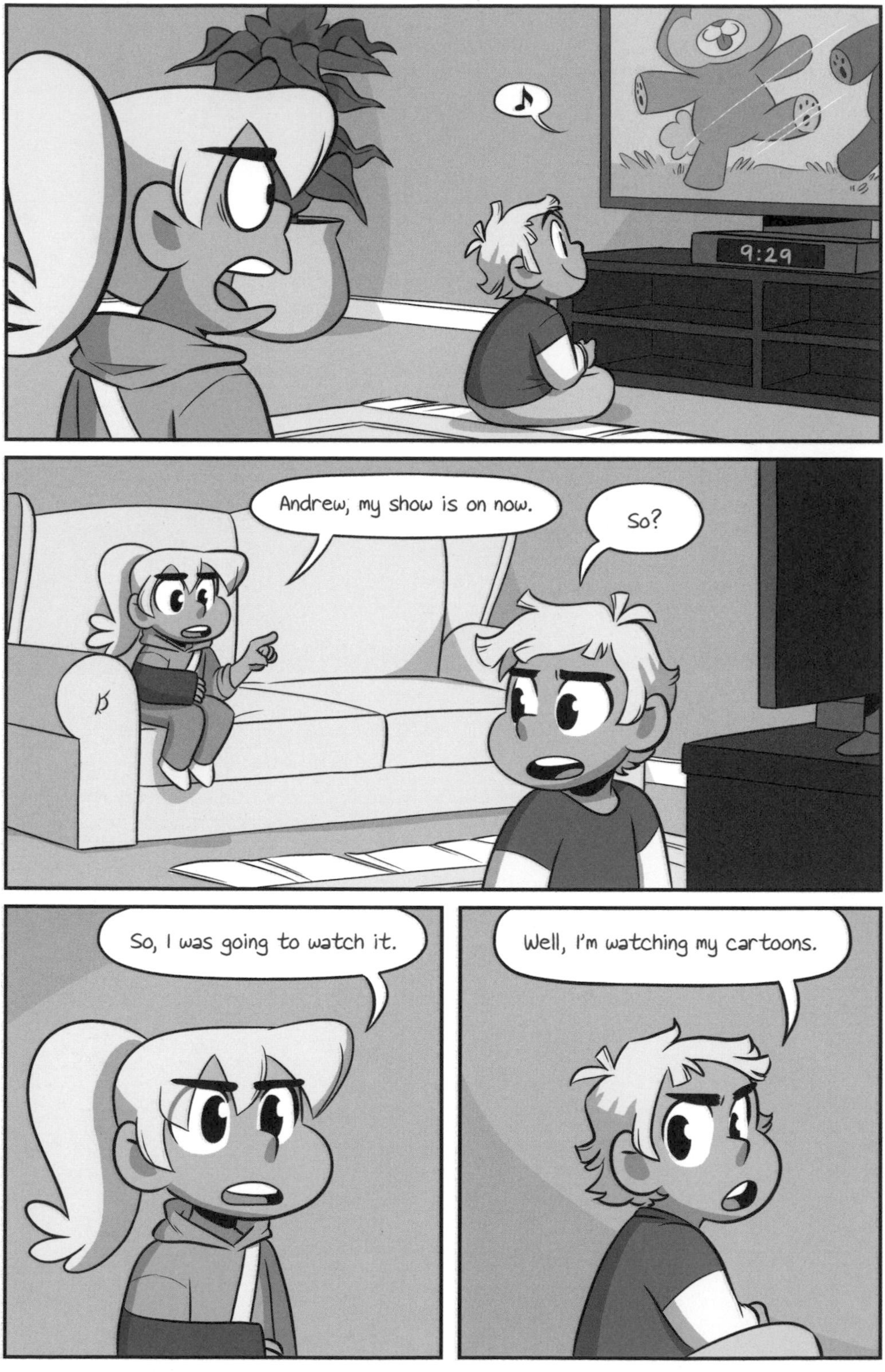
♪
9:29
Andrew, my show is on now.
So?
So, I was going to watch it.
Well, I'm watching my cartoons.

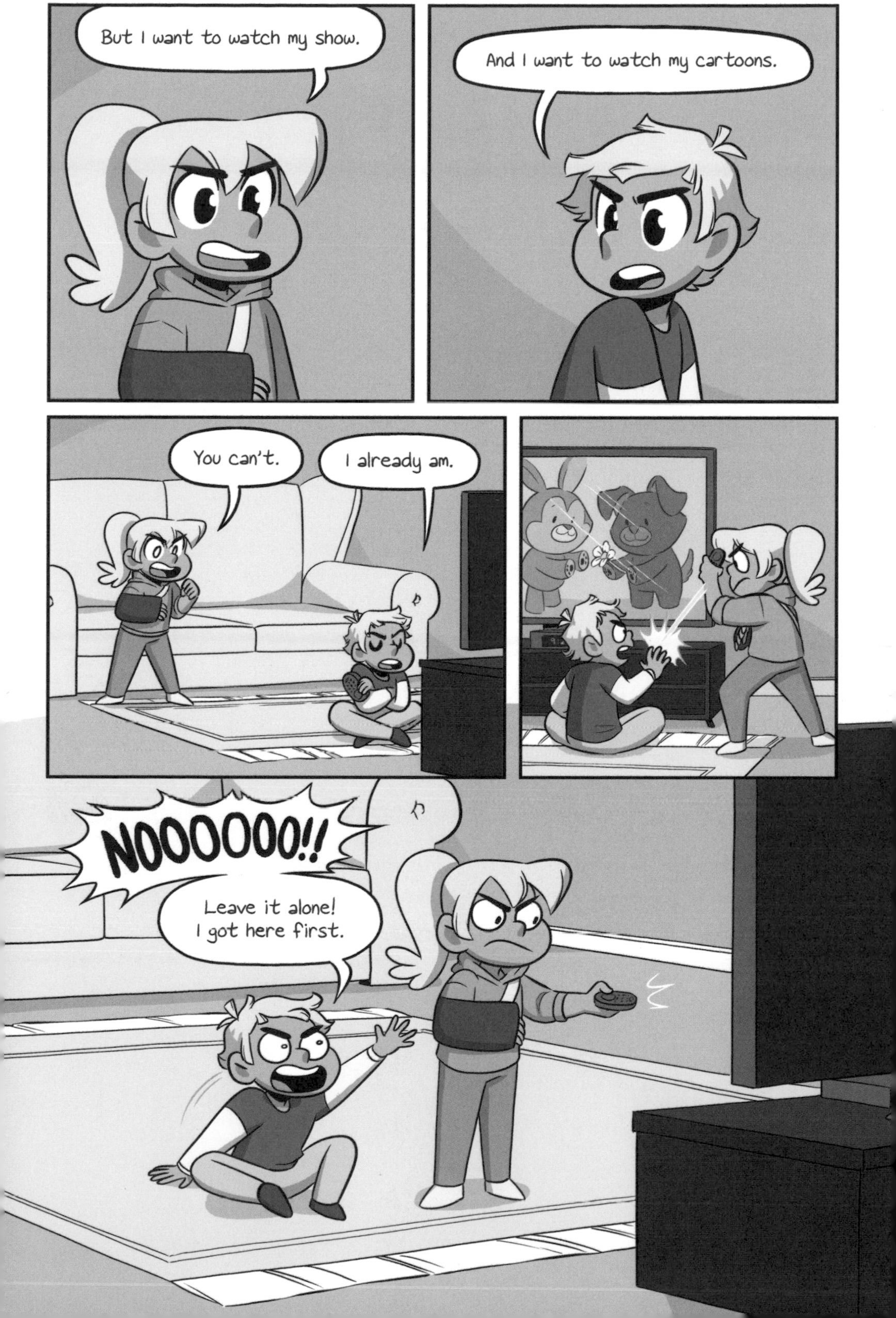
But I want to watch my show.
And I want to watch my cartoons.
You can't.
I already am.
NOOOOOO!!
Leave it alone!
I got here first.

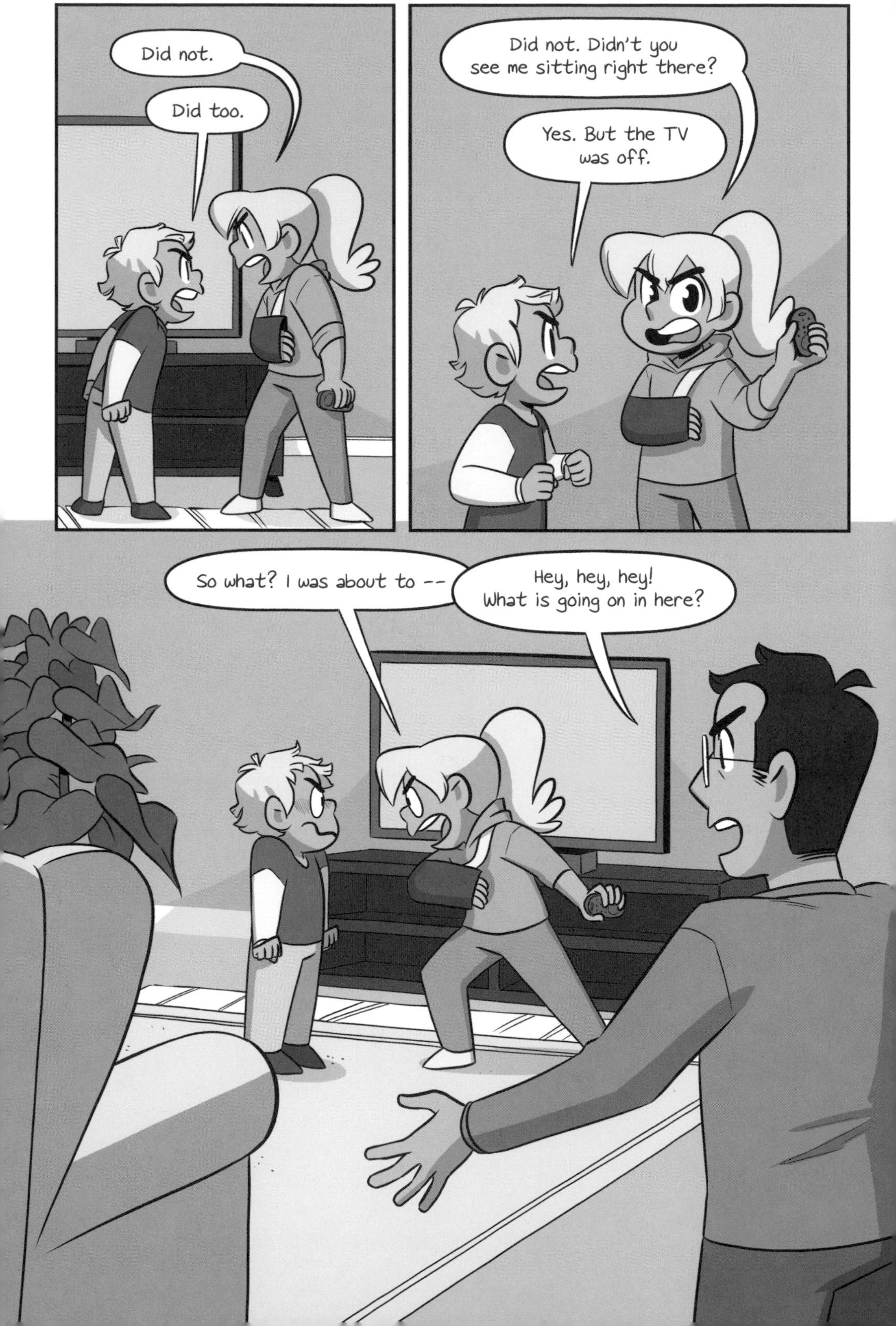
Did not.
Did too.
Did not. Didn't you see me sitting right there?
Yes. But the TV was off.
So what? I was about to --
Hey, hey, hey! What is going on in here?

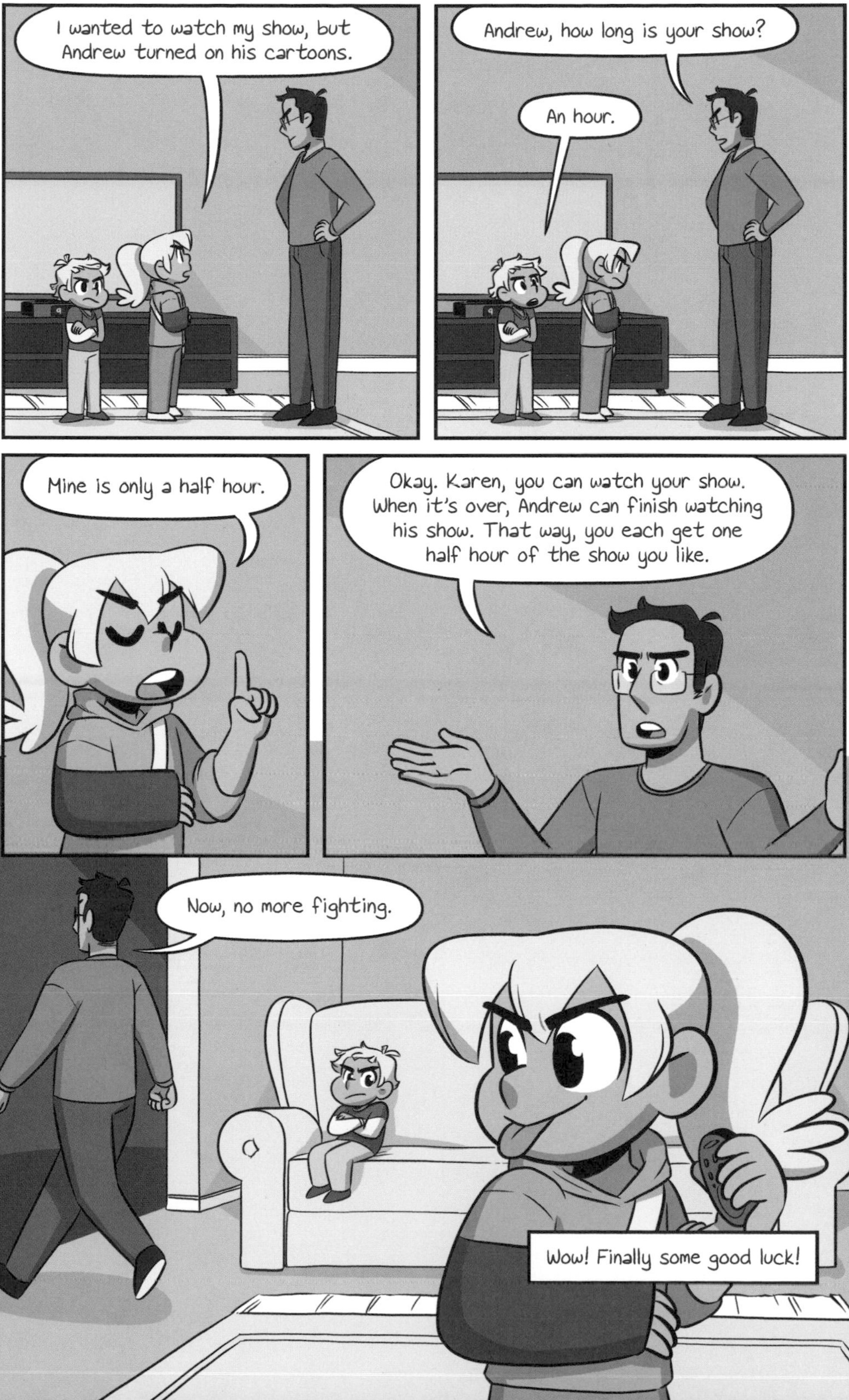
I wanted to watch my show, but Andrew turned on his cartoons.
Andrew, how long is your show?
An hour.
Mine is only a half hour.
Okay. Karen, you can watch your show. When it's over, Andrew can finish watching his show. That way, you each get one half hour of the show you like.
Now, no more fighting.
Wow! Finally some good luck!

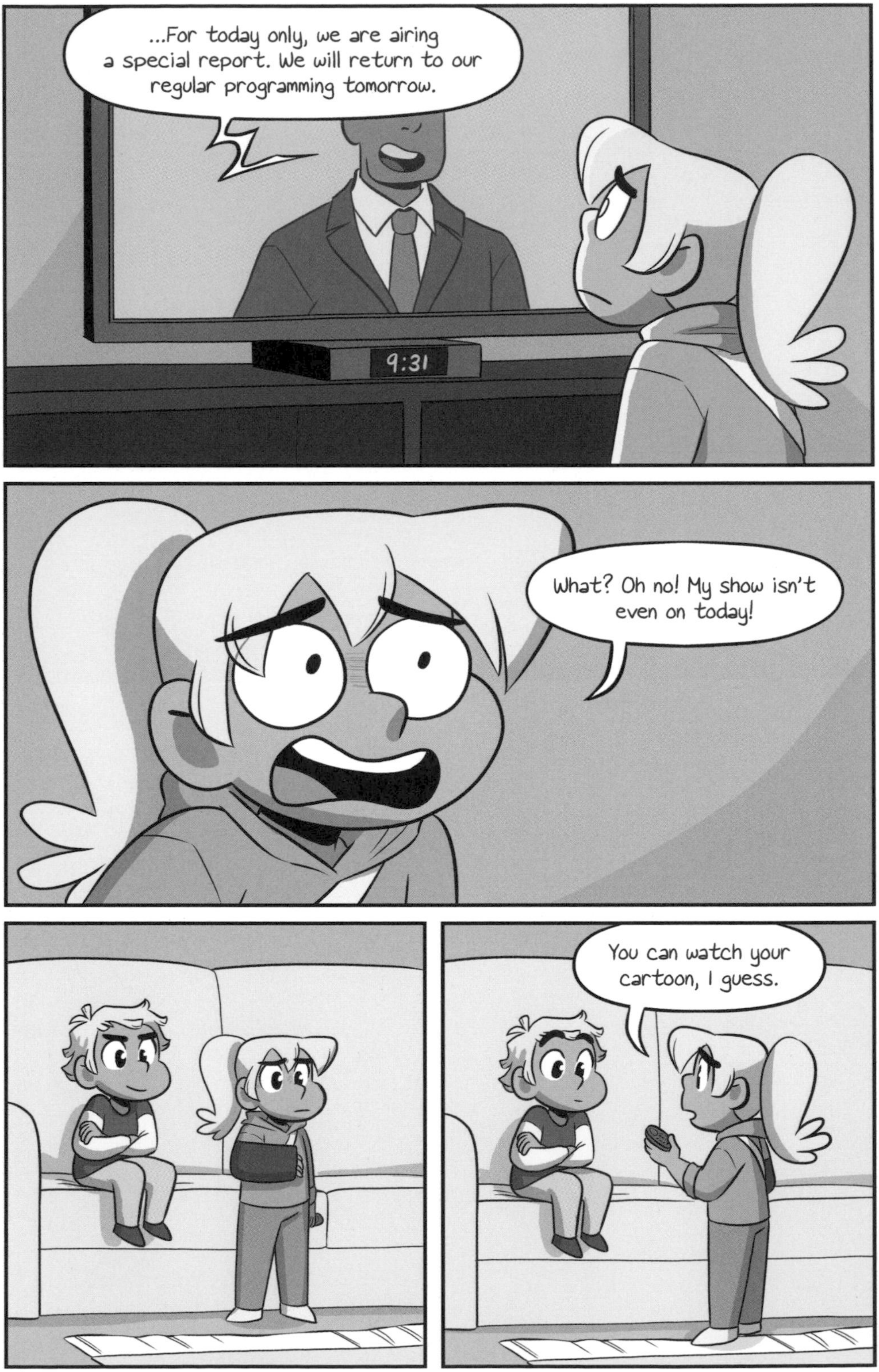
...For today only, we are airing a special report. We will return to our regular programming tomorrow.
9:31
What? Oh no! My show isn't even on today!
You can watch your cartoon, I guess.

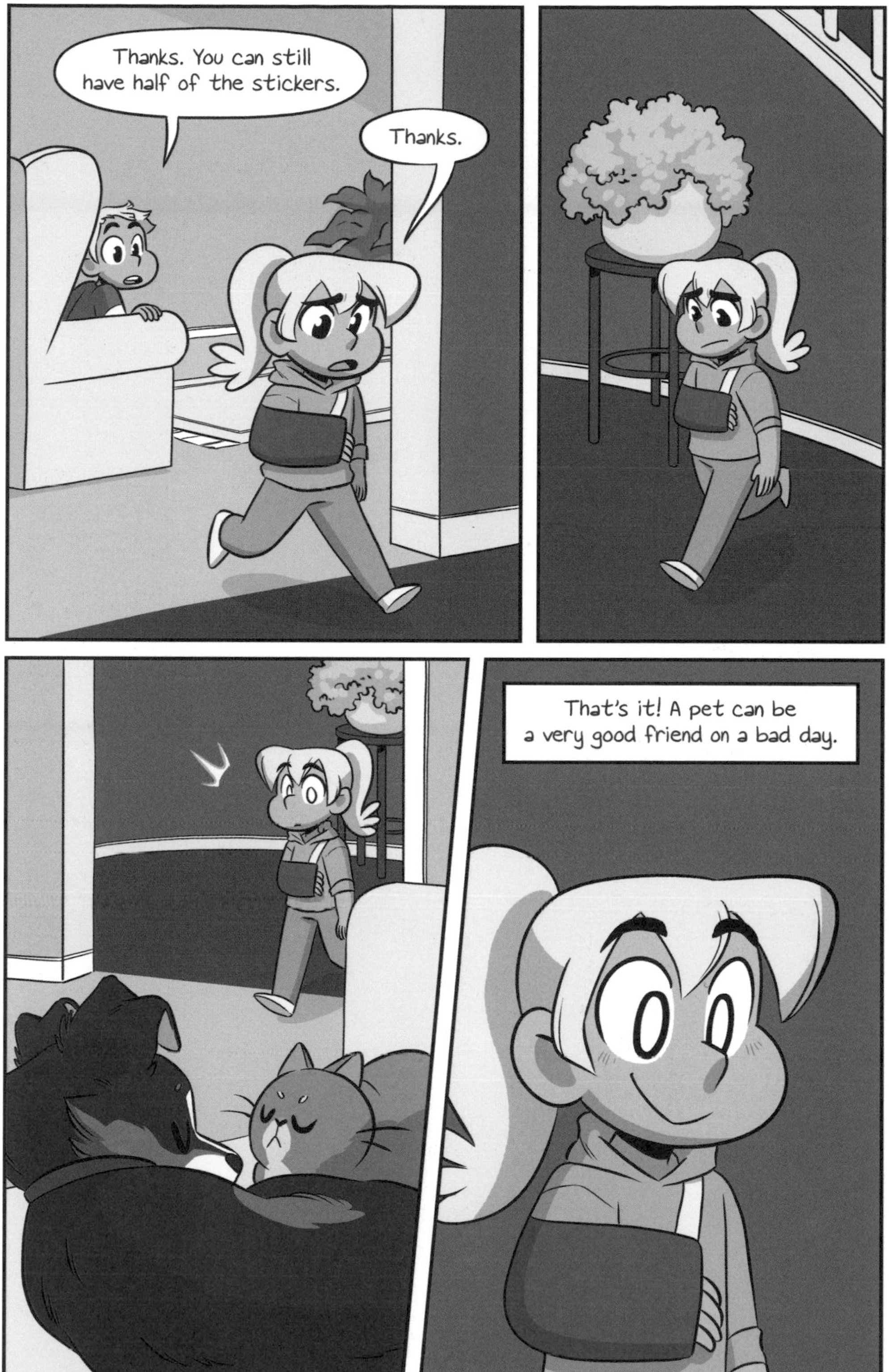
Thanks. You can still have half of the stickers.
Thanks.
That's it! A pet can be a very good friend on a bad day.

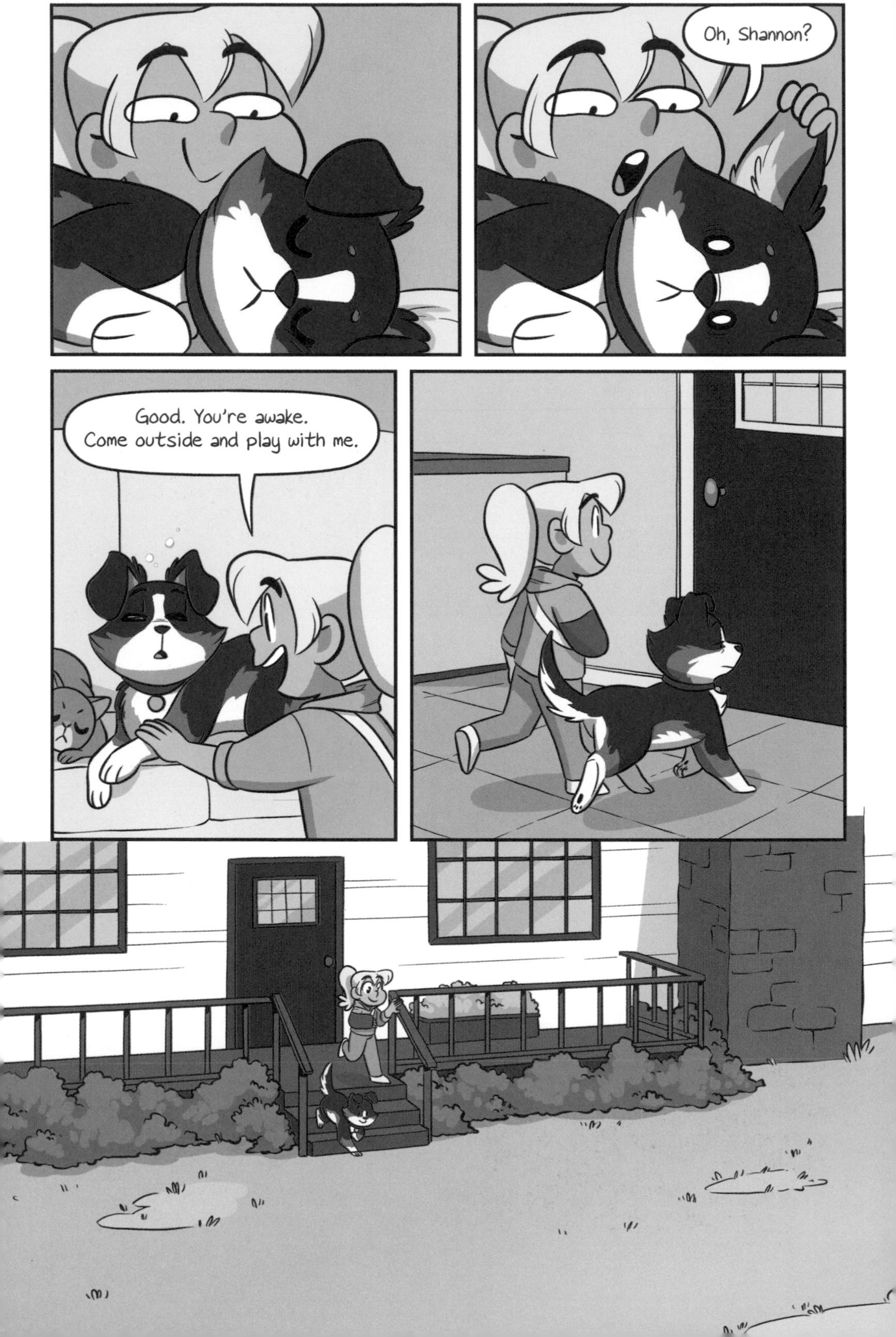
Oh, Shannon?
Good. You're awake.
Come outside and play with me.

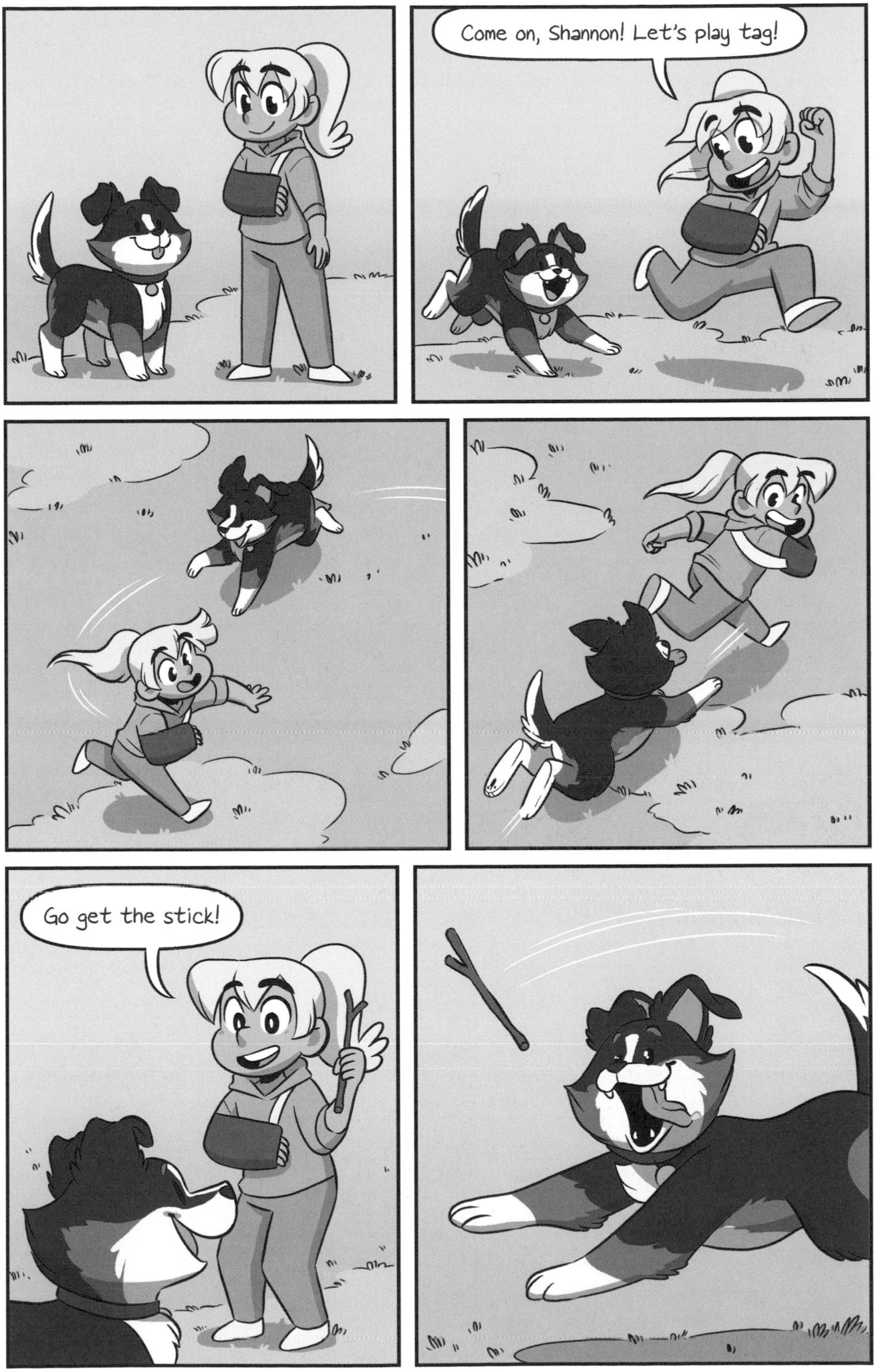
Come on, Shannon! Let's play tag!
Go get the stick!

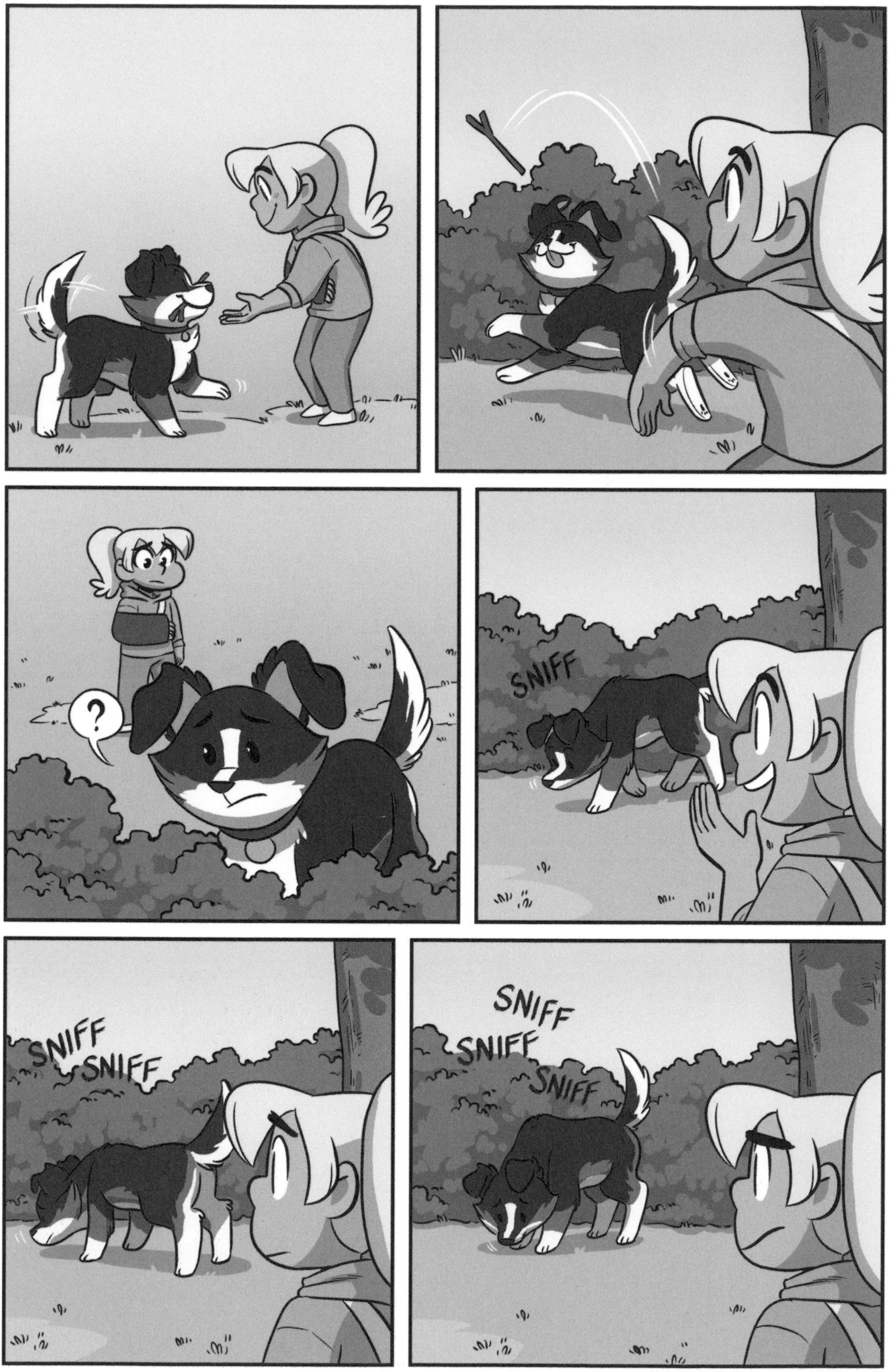
?
SNIFF
SNIFF
SNIFF
SNIFF
SNIFF
SNIFF

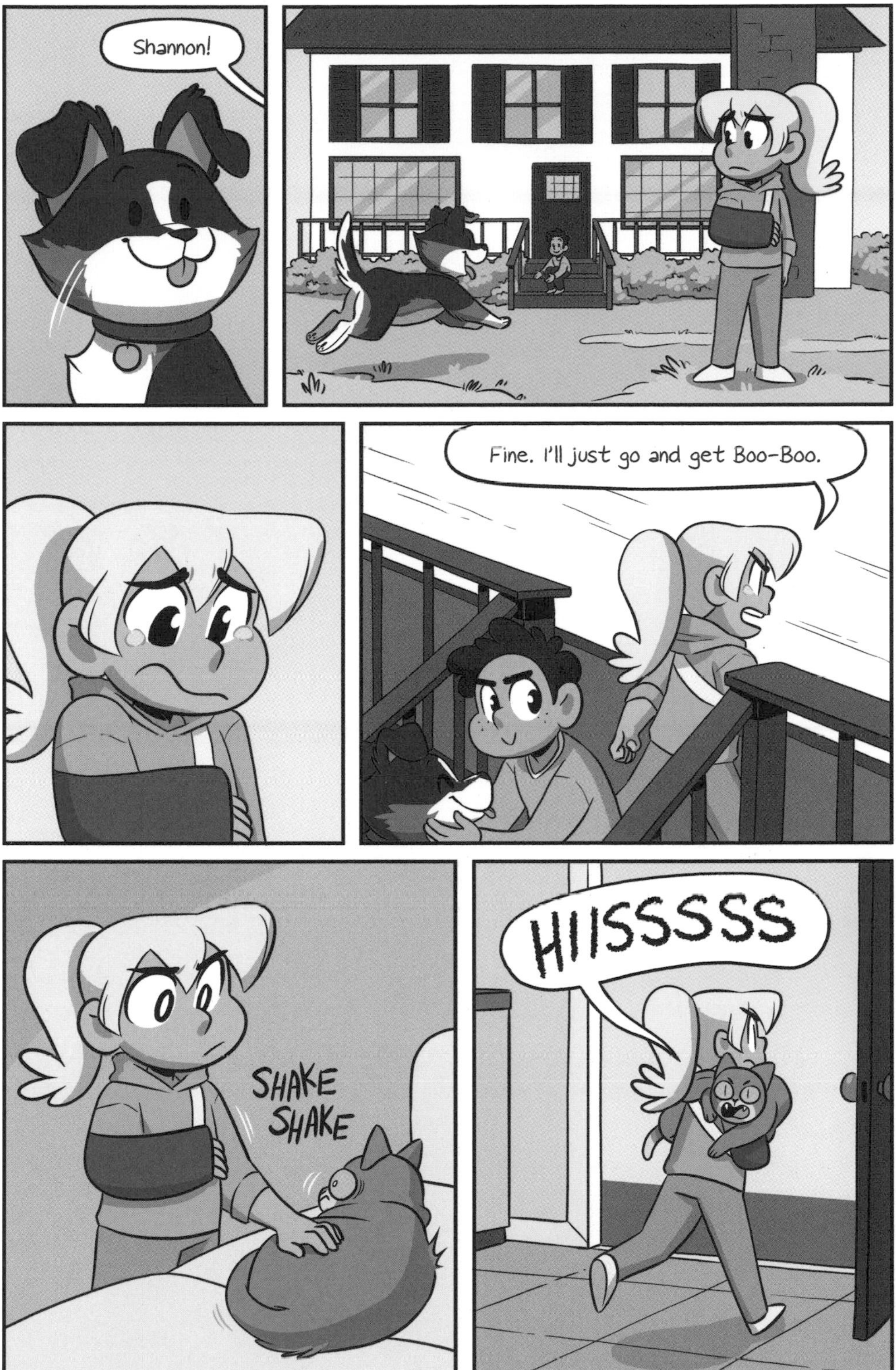
Shannon!
Fine. I'll just go and get Boo-Boo.
SHAKE SHAKE
HIISSSSS

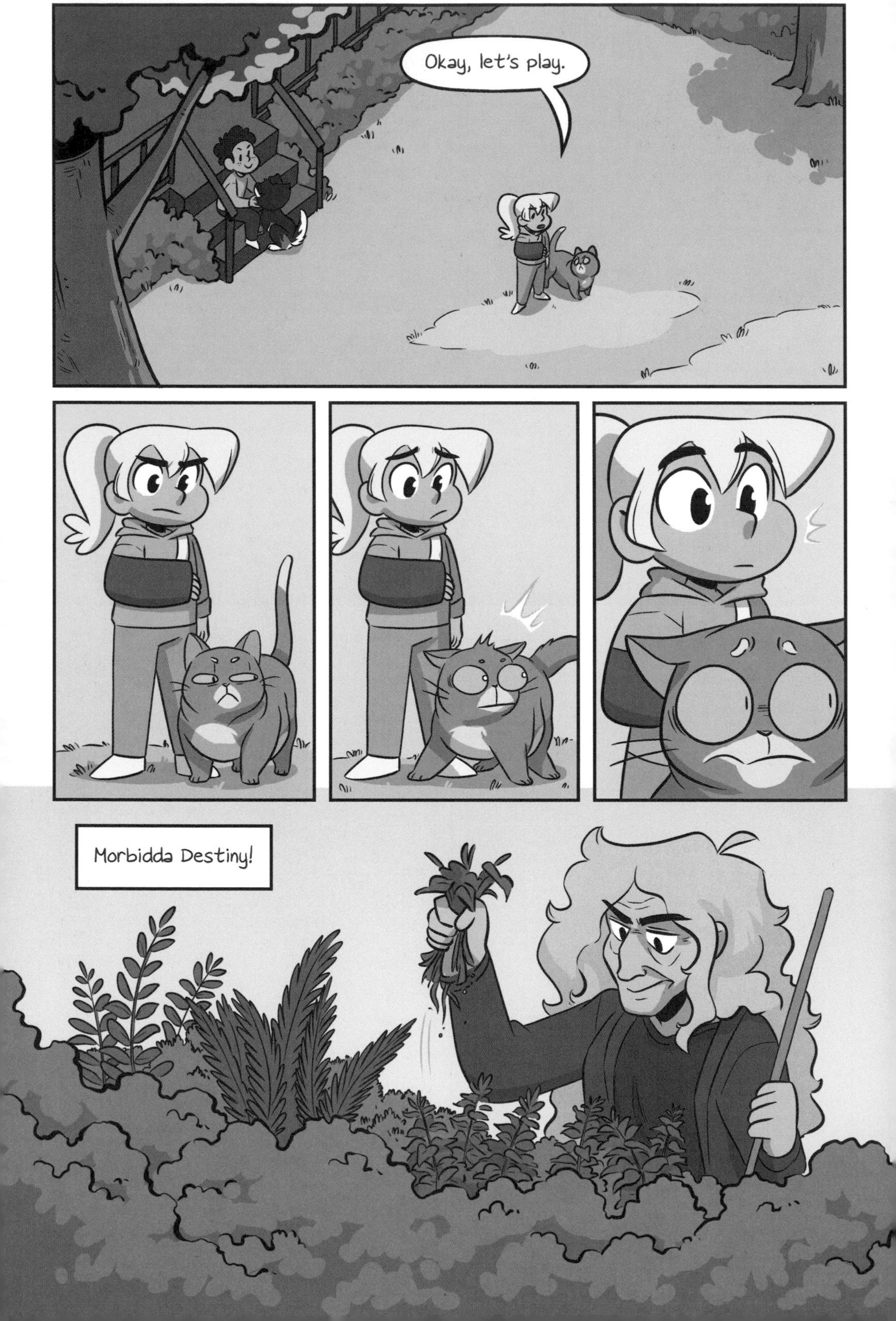
Okay, let's play.
Morbidda Destiny!

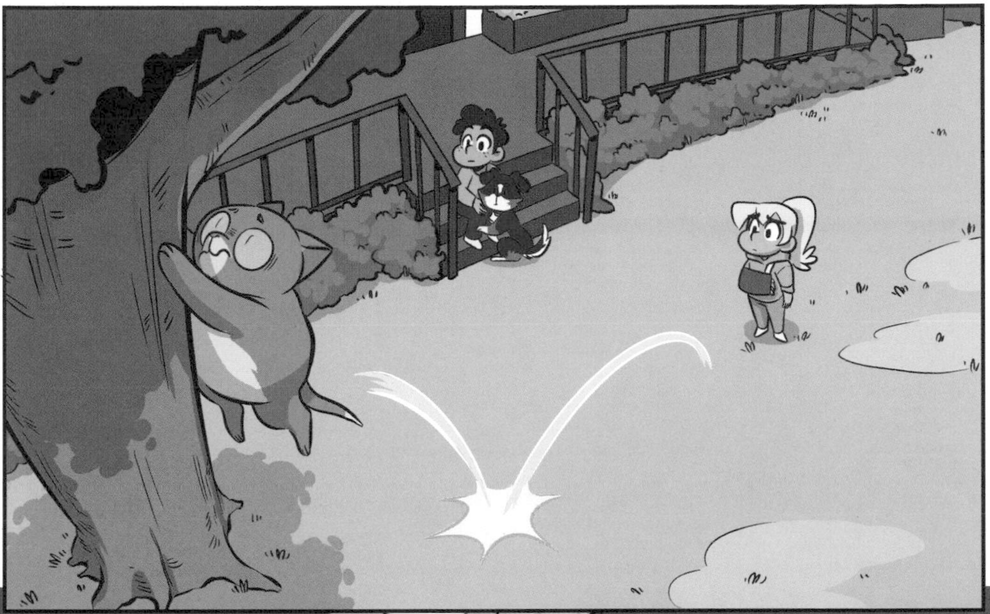

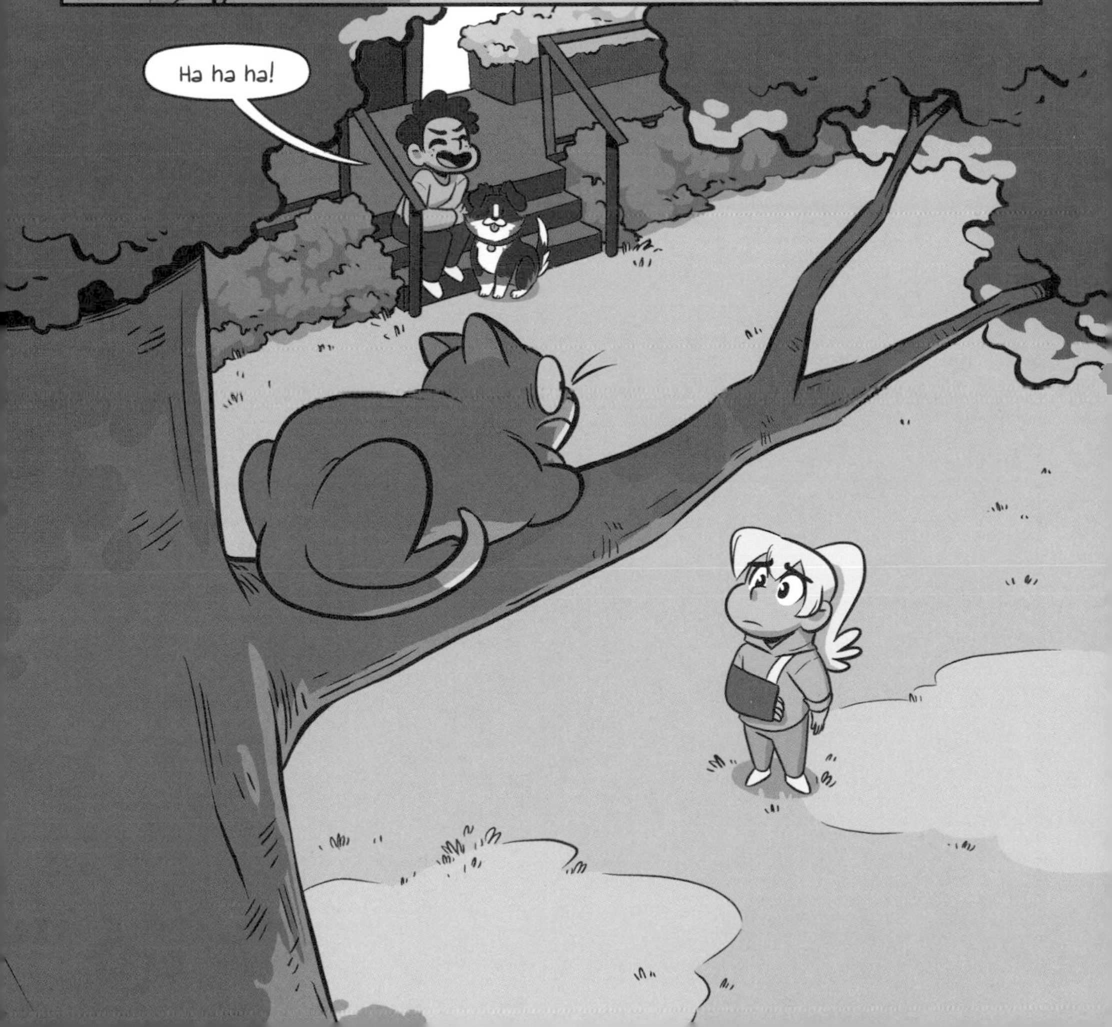
Ha ha ha!

CHAPTER 4

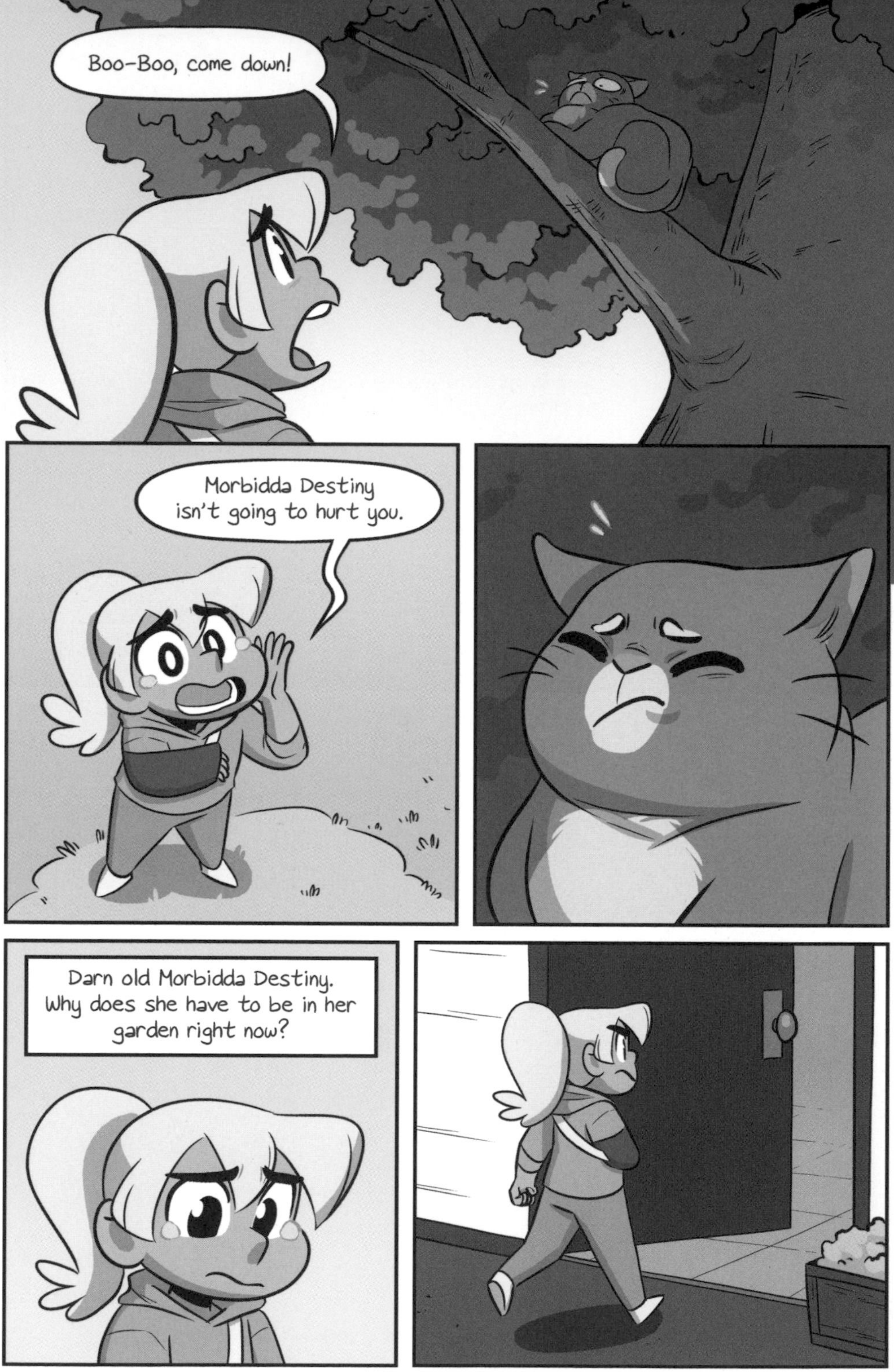

Boo-Boo, come down!
Morbidda Destiny isn't going to hurt you.
Darn old Morbidda Destiny. Why does she have to be in her garden right now?

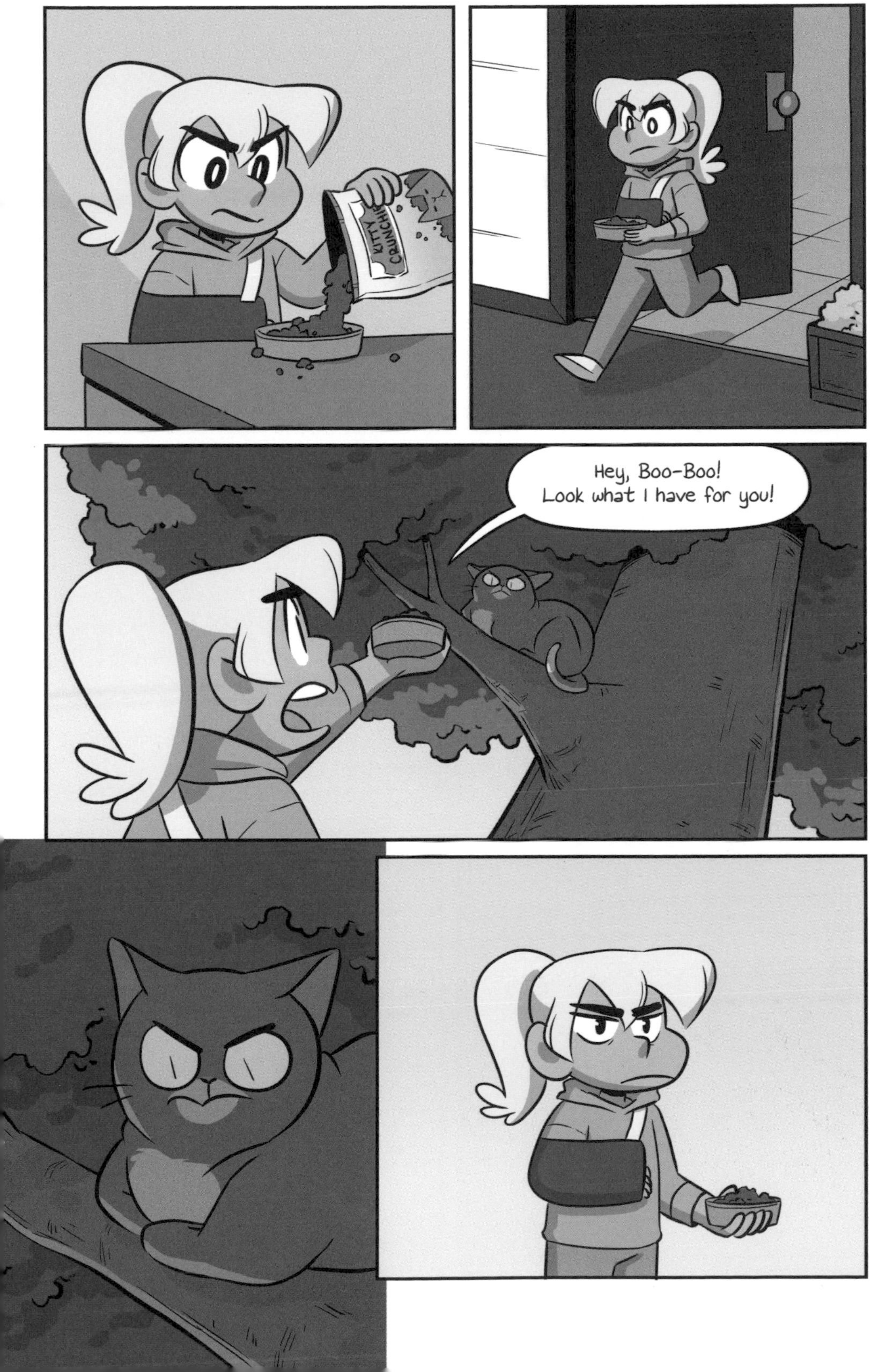
KITTY CRUNCHIES
Hey, Boo-Boo! Look what I have for you!

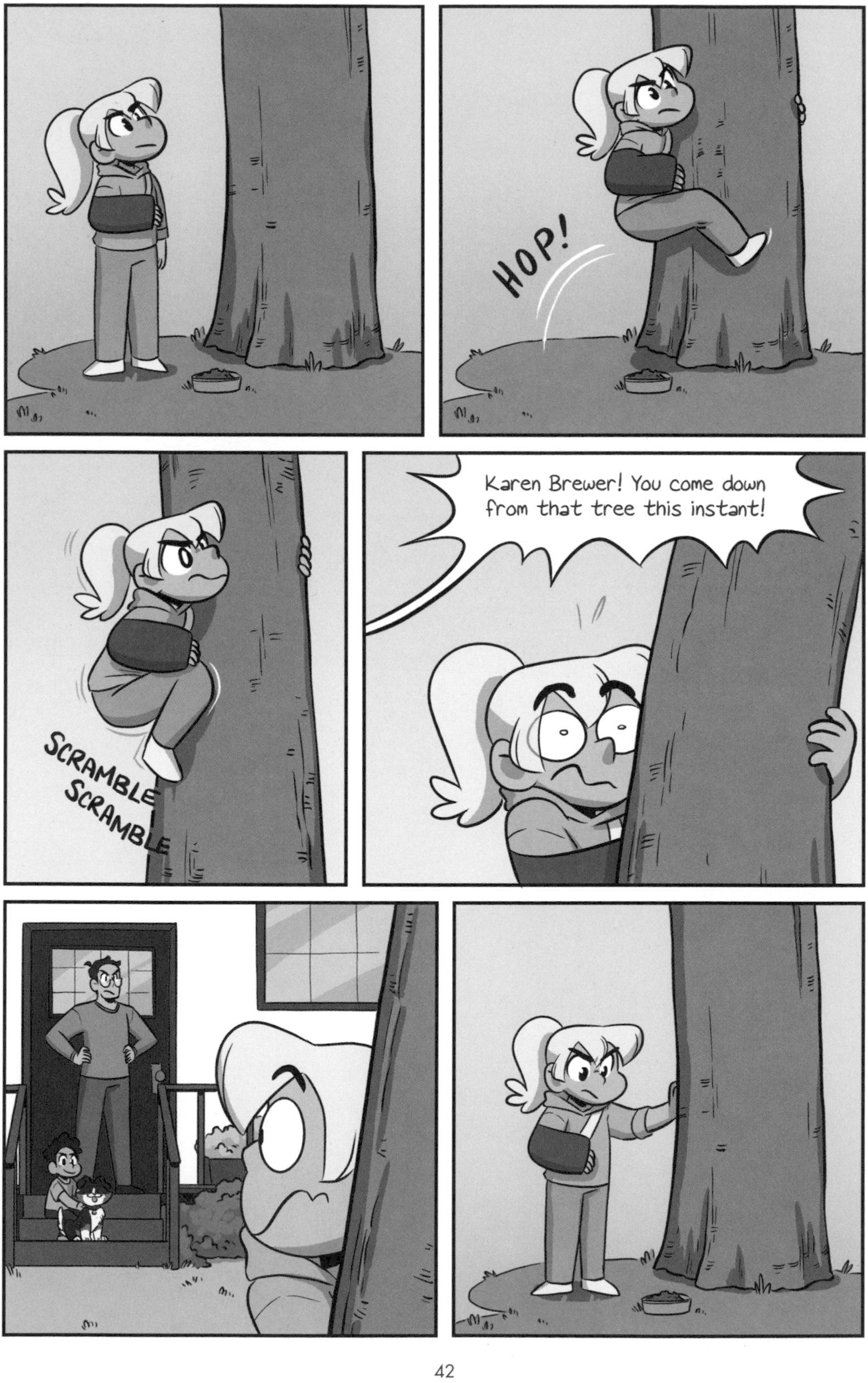
HOP!
SCRAMBLE
SCRAMBLE
Karen Brewer! You come down from that tree this instant!

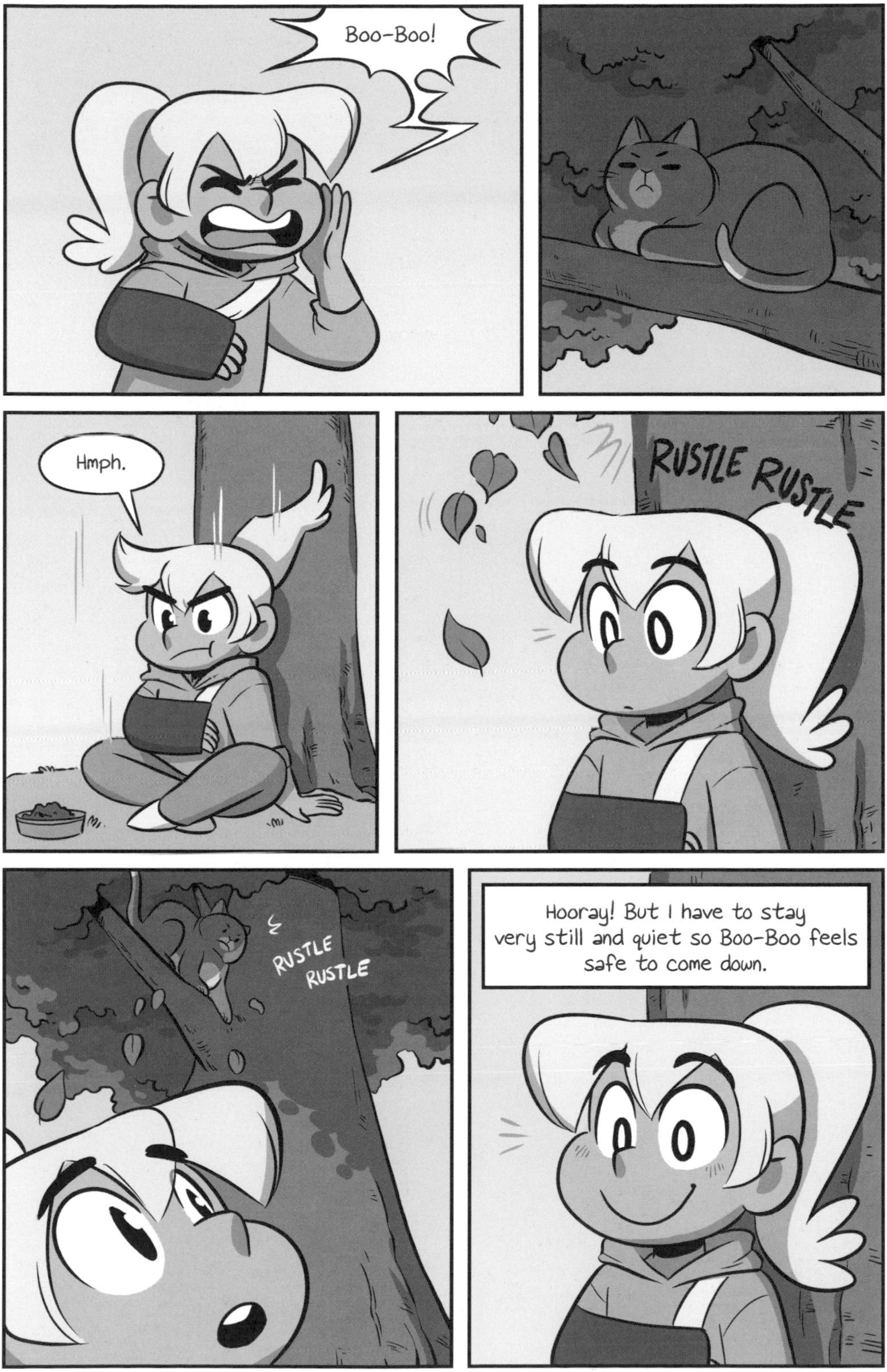
Boo-Boo!
Hmph.
RUSTLE RUSTLE
RUSTLE RUSTLE
Hooray! But I have to stay very still and quiet so Boo-Boo feels safe to come down.

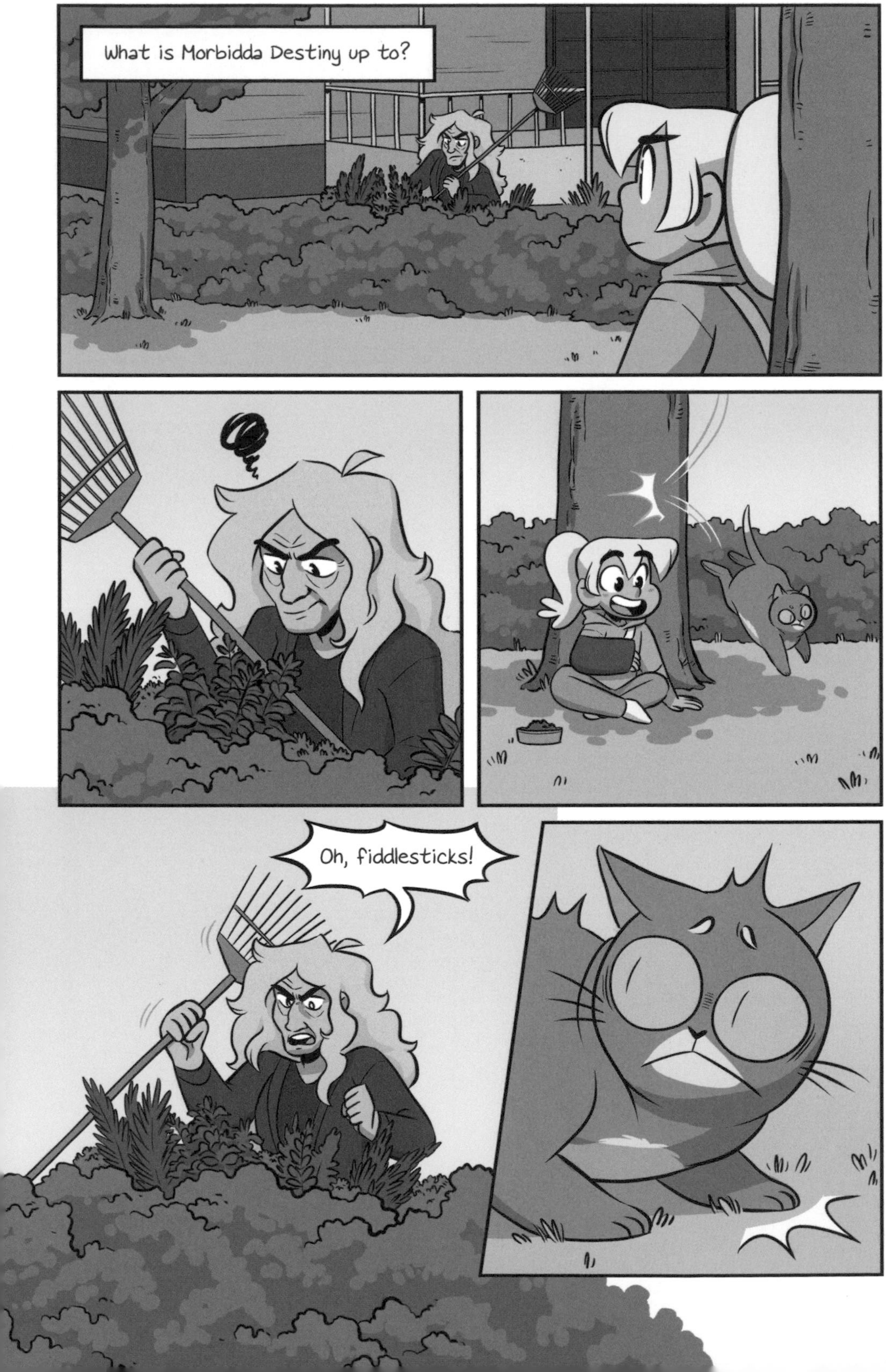
What is Morbidda Destiny up to?
Oh, fiddlesticks!

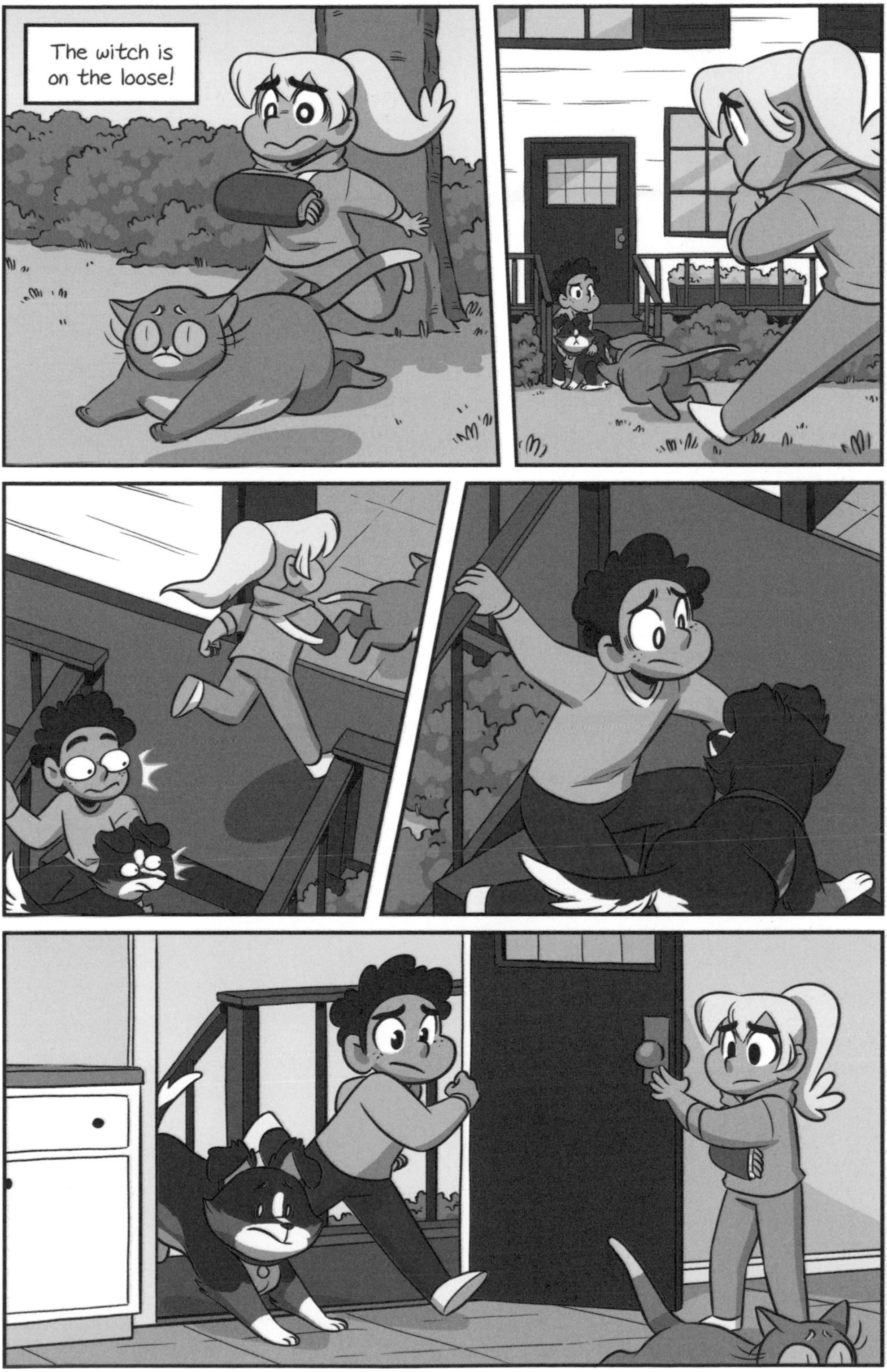
The witch is
on the loose!

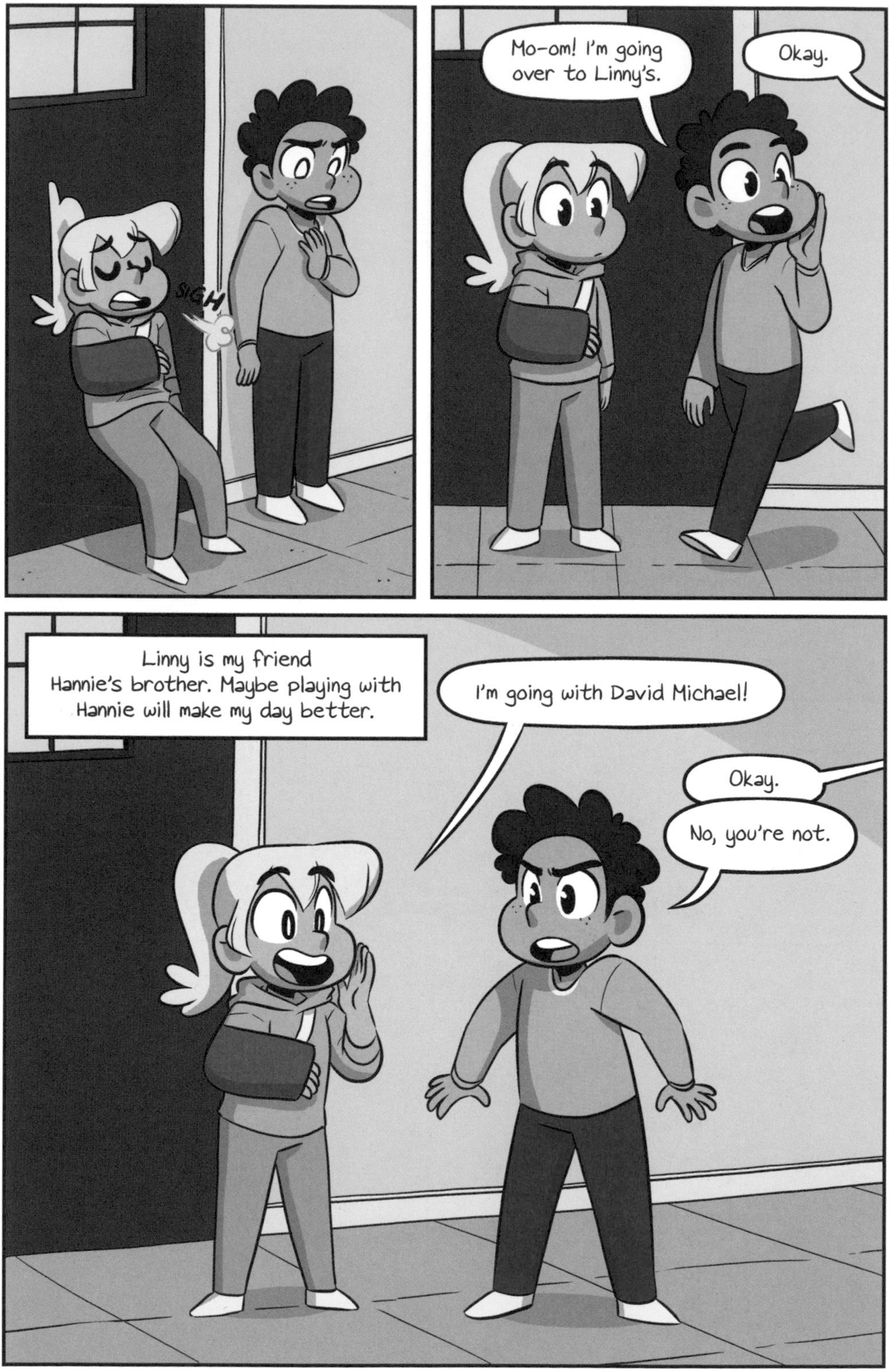
SIGH
Mo-om! I'm going over to Linny's.
Okay.
Linny is my friend Hannie's brother. Maybe playing with Hannie will make my day better.
I'm going with David Michael!
Okay.
No, you're not.

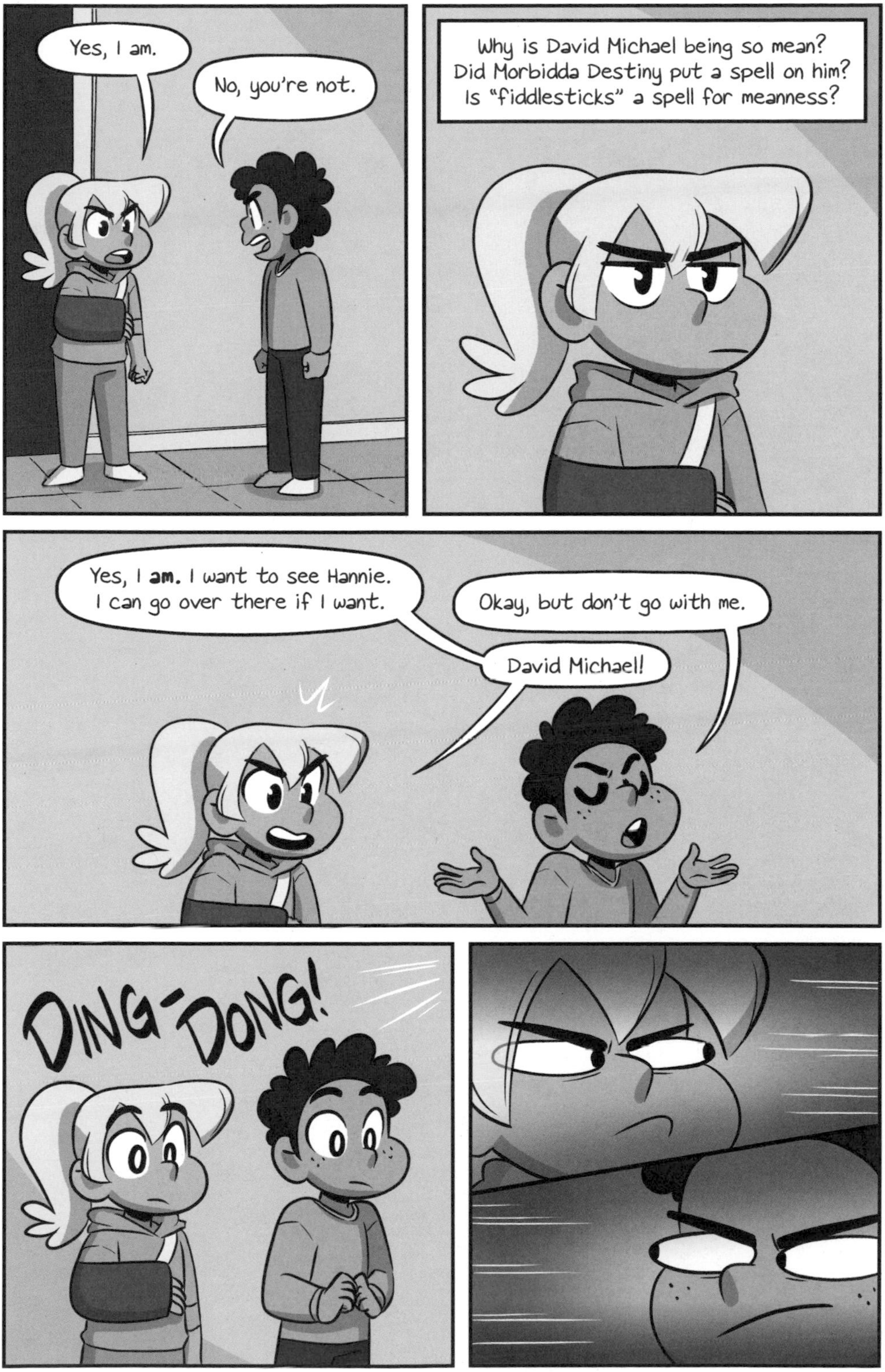

Yes, I am.
No, you're not.
Why is David Michael being so mean? Did Morbidda Destiny put a spell on him? Is "fiddlesticks" a spell for meanness?
Yes, I **am.** I want to see Hannie. I can go over there if I want.
Okay, but don't go with me.
David Michael!
DING-DONG!

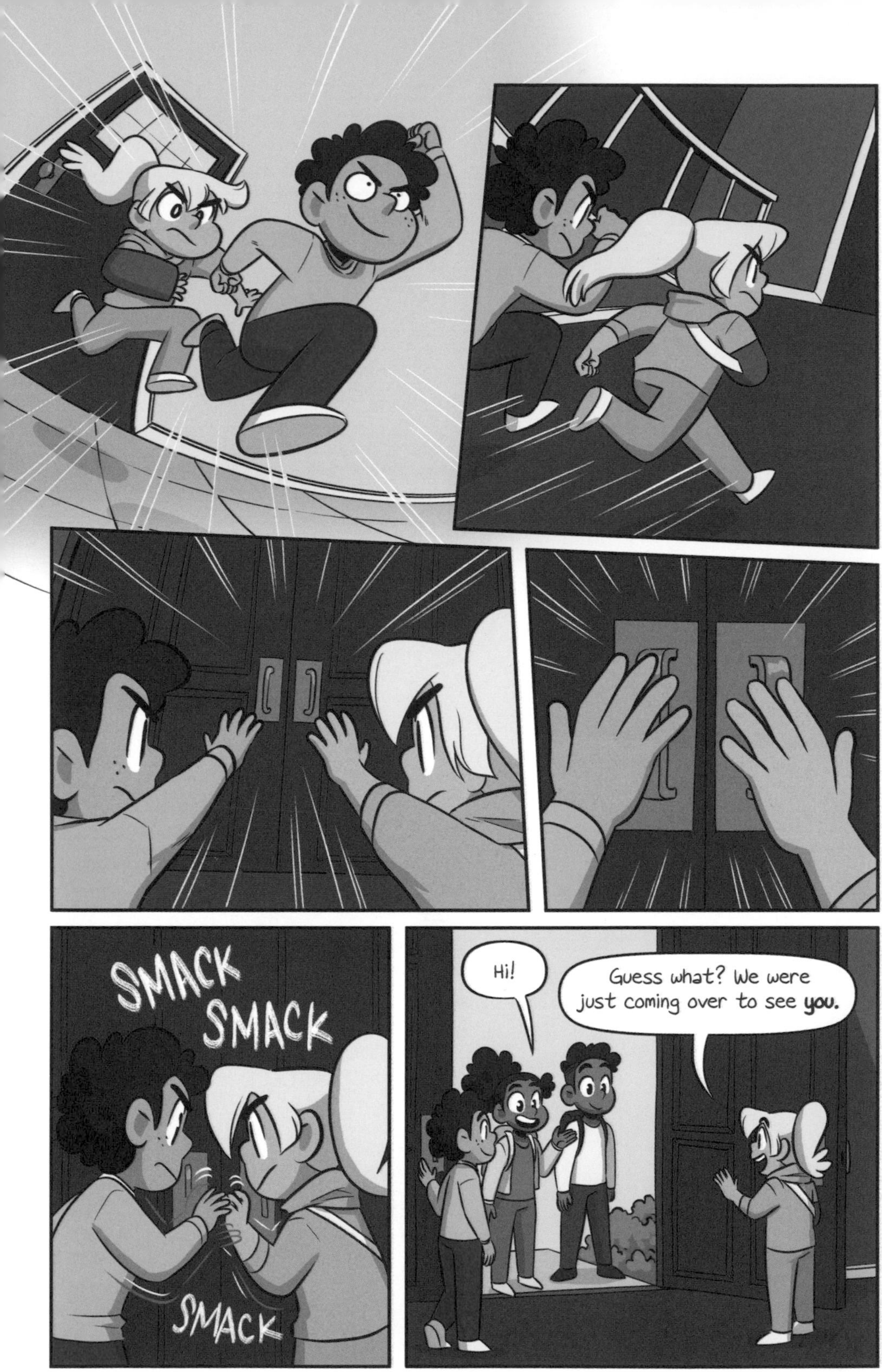
SMACK
SMACK
SMACK
Hi!
Guess what? We were just coming over to see **you.**

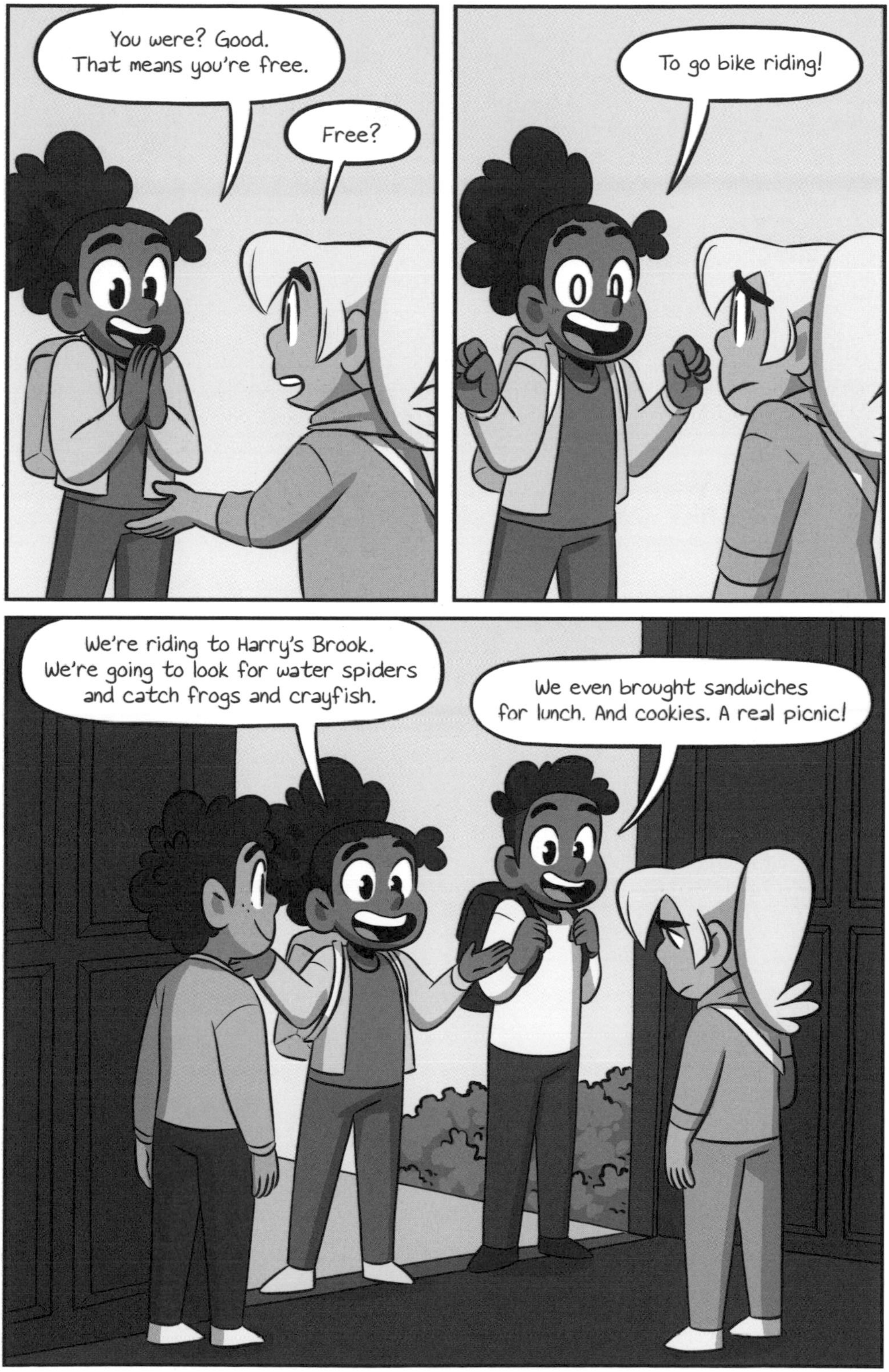
You were? Good. That means you're free.
Free?
To go bike riding!
We're riding to Harry's Brook. We're going to look for water spiders and catch frogs and crayfish.
We even brought sandwiches for lunch. And cookies. A real picnic!

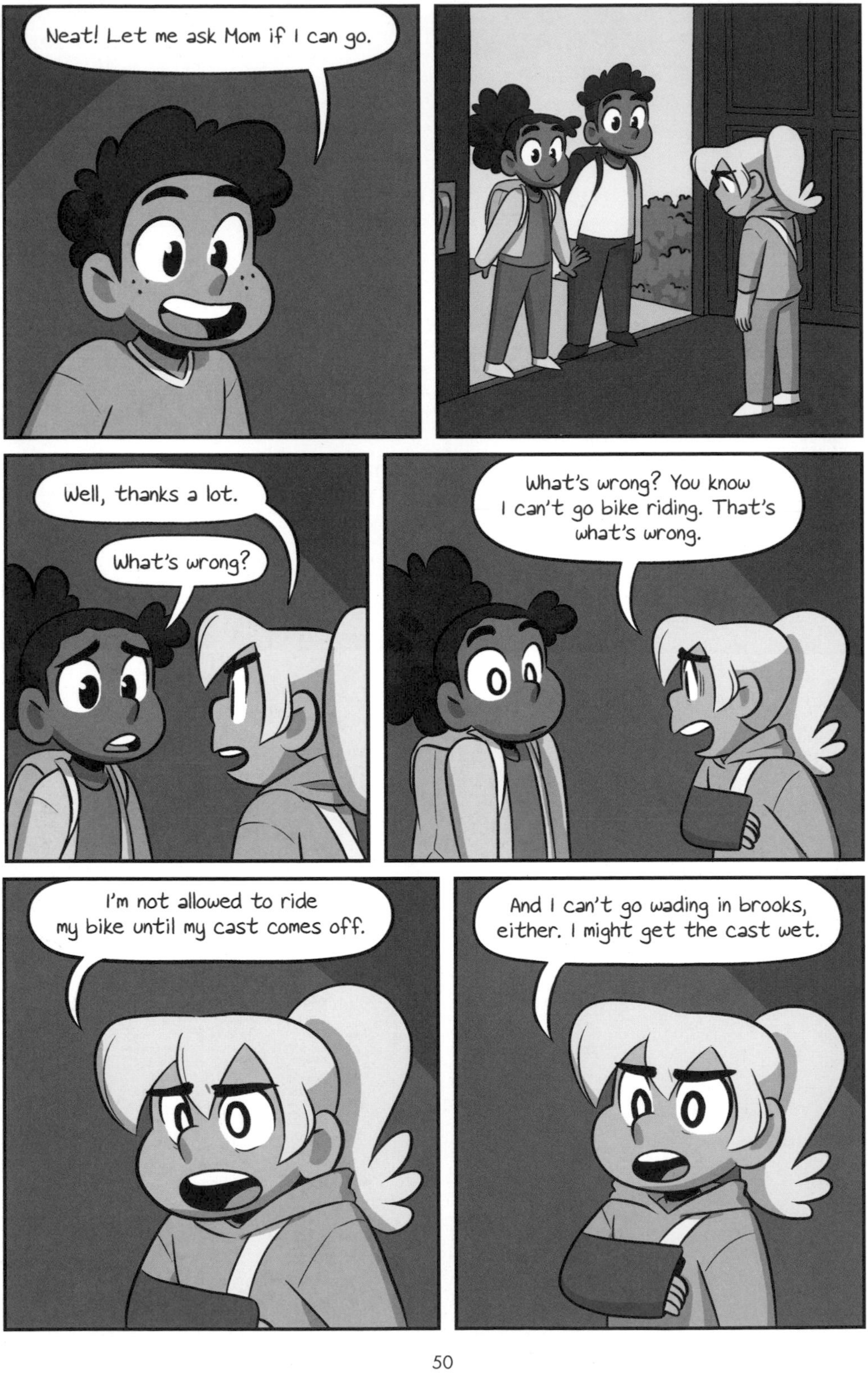
Neat! Let me ask Mom if I can go.
Well, thanks a lot.
What's wrong?
What's wrong? You know I can't go bike riding. That's what's wrong.
I'm not allowed to ride my bike until my cast comes off.
And I can't go wading in brooks, either. I might get the cast wet.

CHAPTER 5

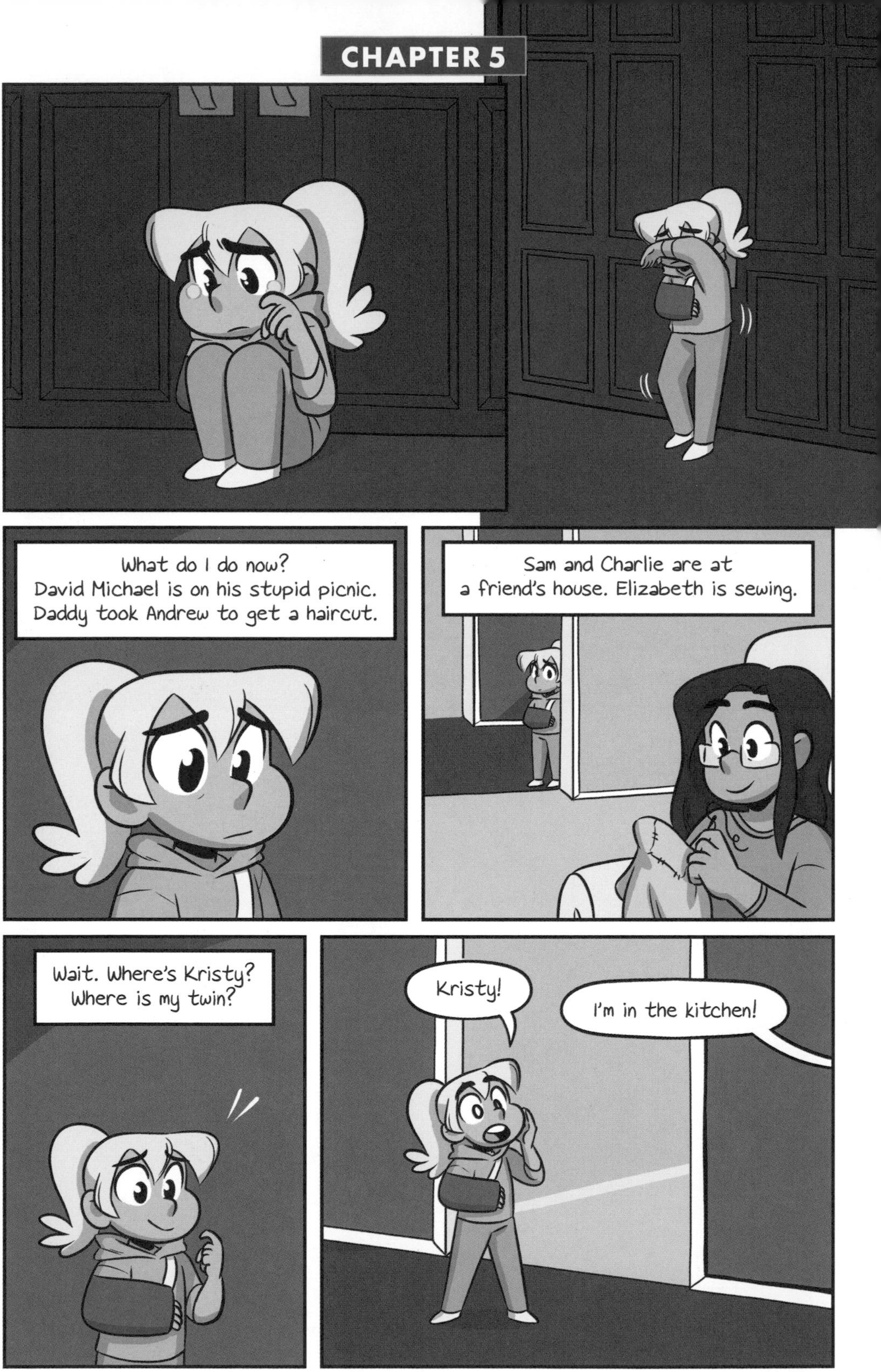

What do I do now?
David Michael is on his stupid picnic.
Daddy took Andrew to get a haircut.
Sam and Charlie are at a friend's house. Elizabeth is sewing.
Wait. Where's Kristy? Where is my twin?
Kristy!
I'm in the kitchen!

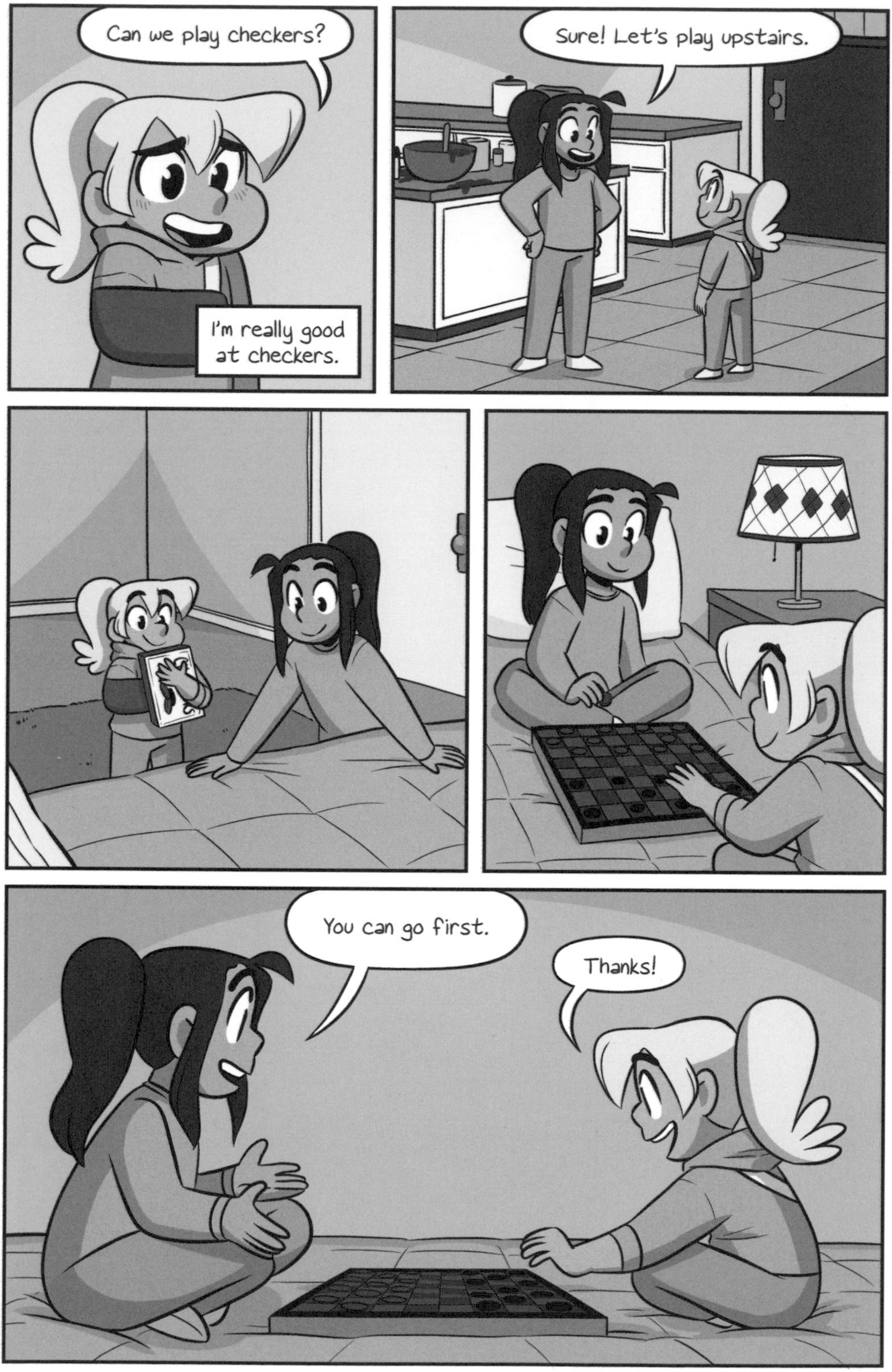
Can we play checkers?
I'm really good at checkers.
Sure! Let's play upstairs.
You can go first.
Thanks!

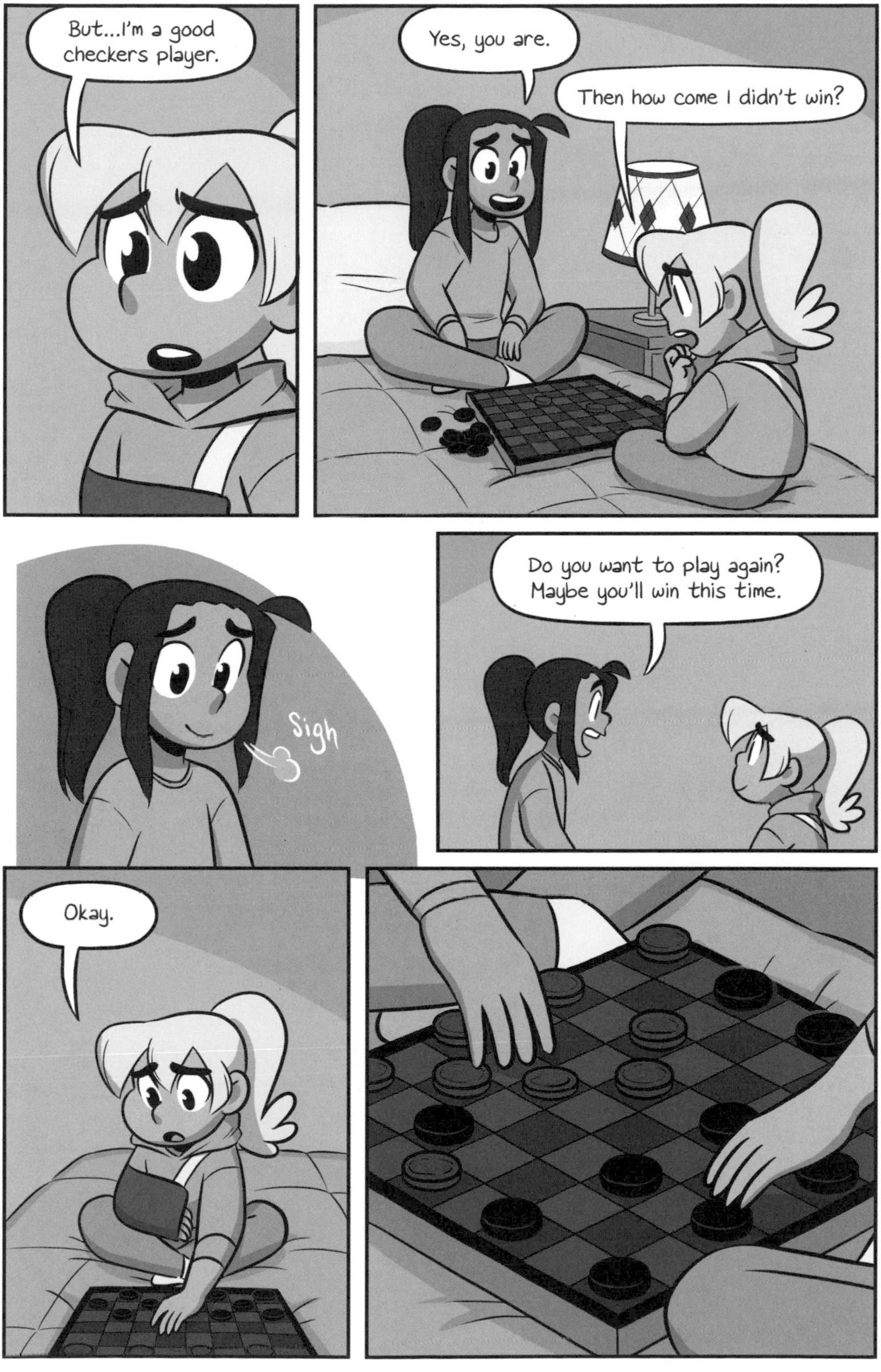
But...I'm a good checkers player.
Yes, you are.
Then how come I didn't win?
Sigh
Do you want to play again? Maybe you'll win this time.
Okay.

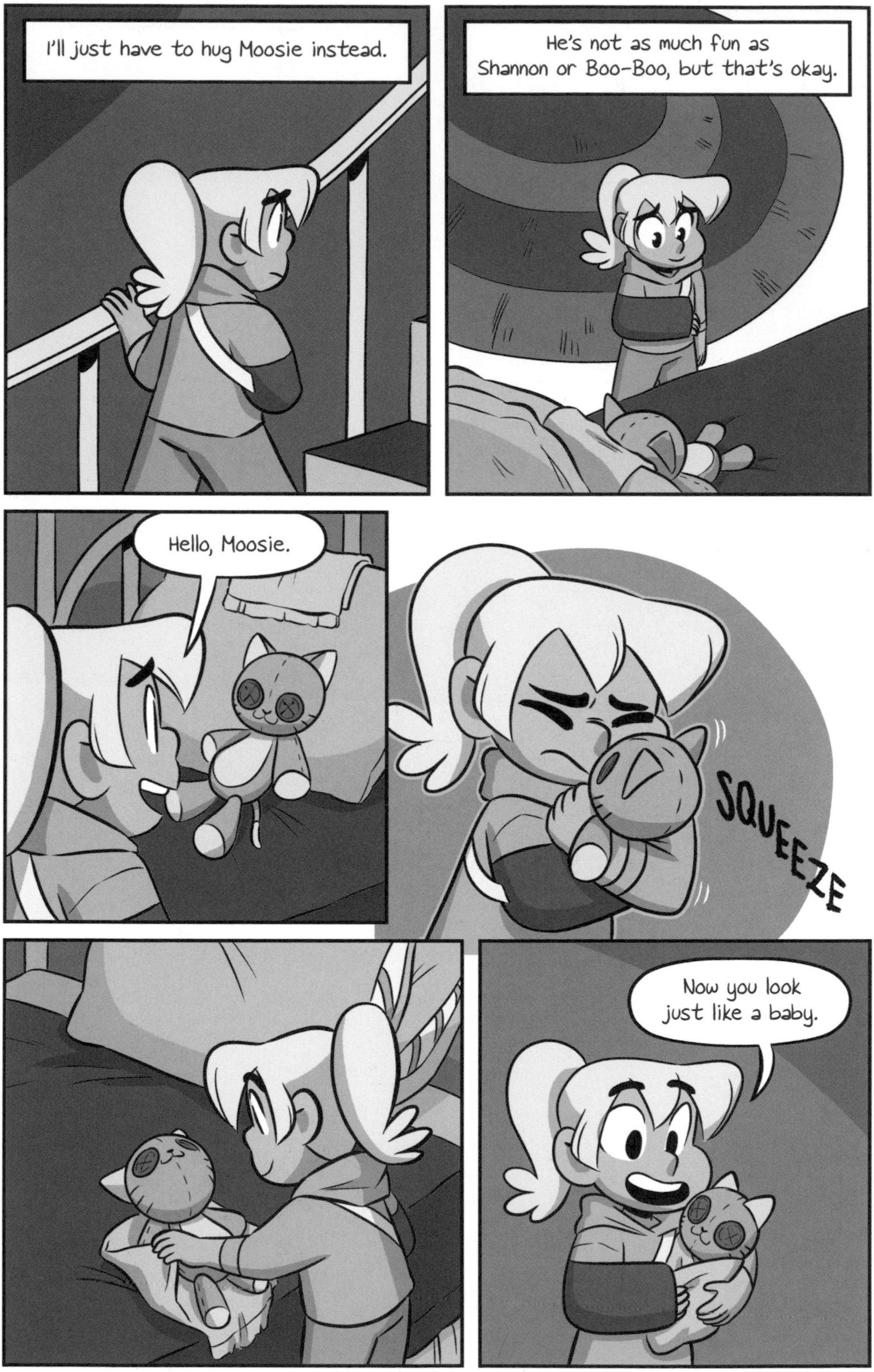
I'll just have to hug Moosie instead.
He's not as much fun as Shannon or Boo-Boo, but that's okay.
Hello, Moosie.
SQUEEZE
Now you look just like a baby.

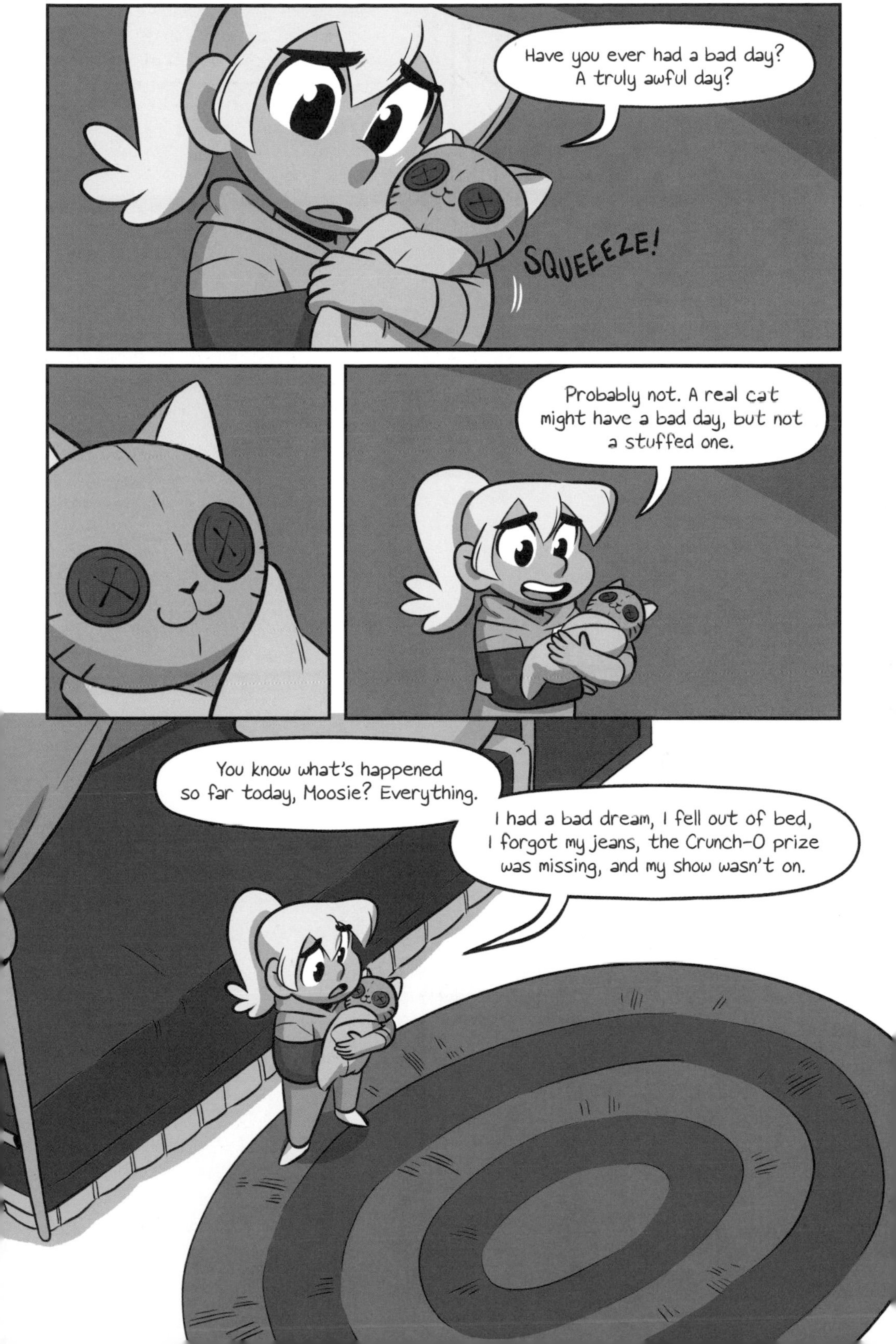
Have you ever had a bad day? A truly awful day?
SQUEEEEZE!
Probably not. A real cat might have a bad day, but not a stuffed one.
You know what's happened so far today, Moosie? Everything.
I had a bad dream, I fell out of bed, I forgot my jeans, the Crunch-O prize was missing, and my show wasn't on.

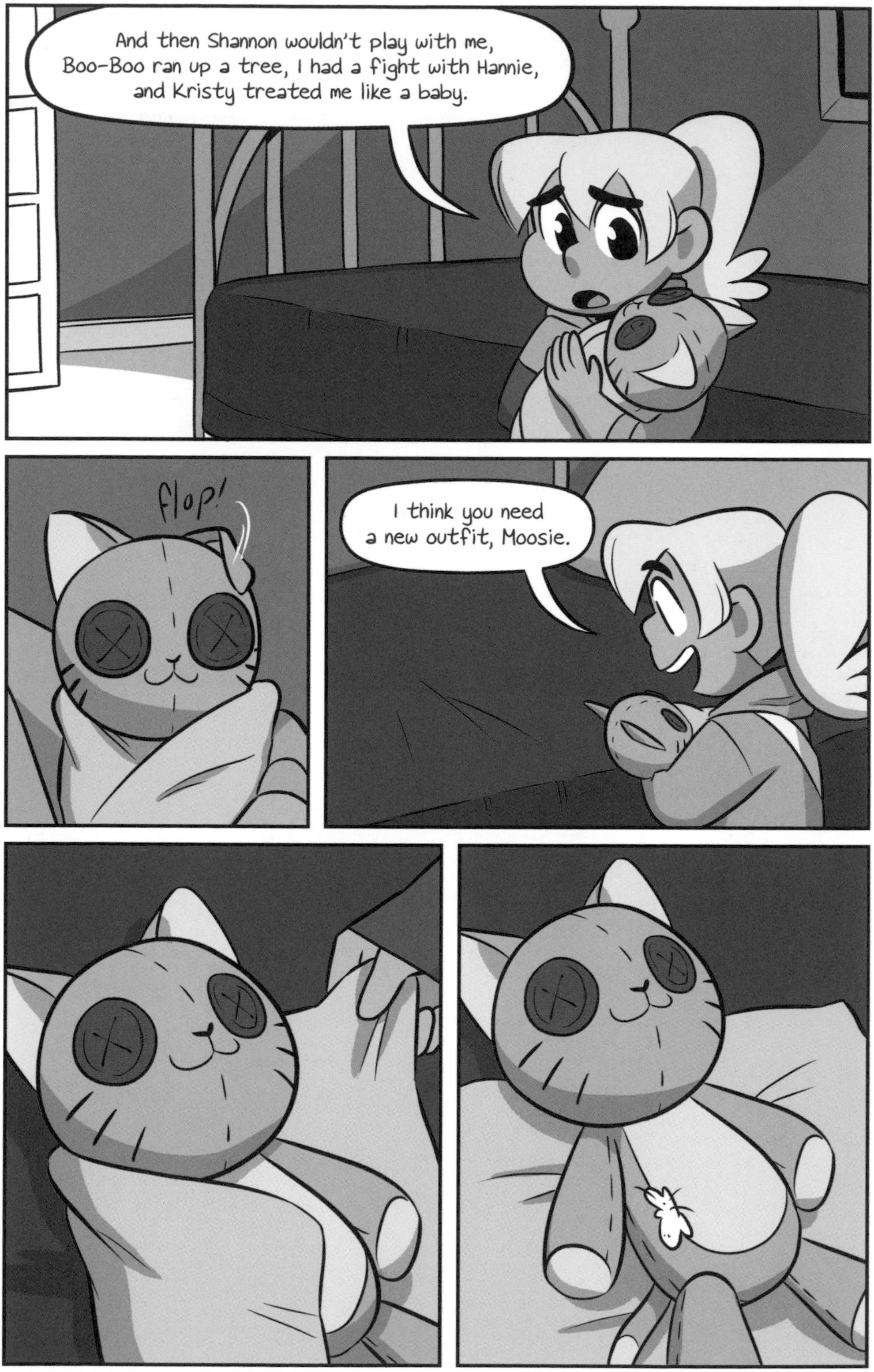
And then Shannon wouldn't play with me, Boo-Boo ran up a tree, I had a fight with Hannie, and Kristy treated me like a baby.
flop!
I think you need a new outfit, Moosie.

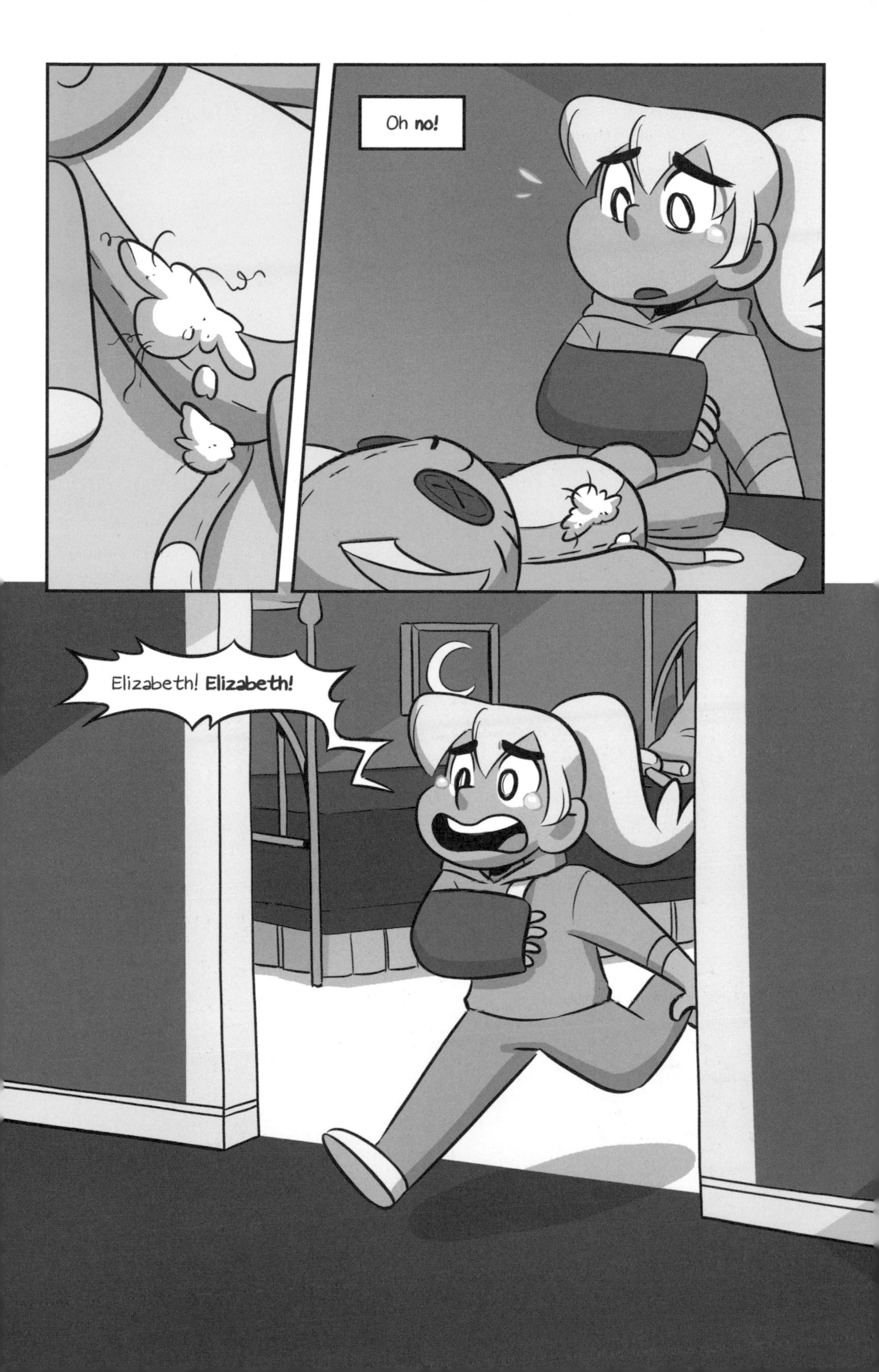
Oh **no!**
Elizabeth! **Elizabeth!**

CHAPTER 6

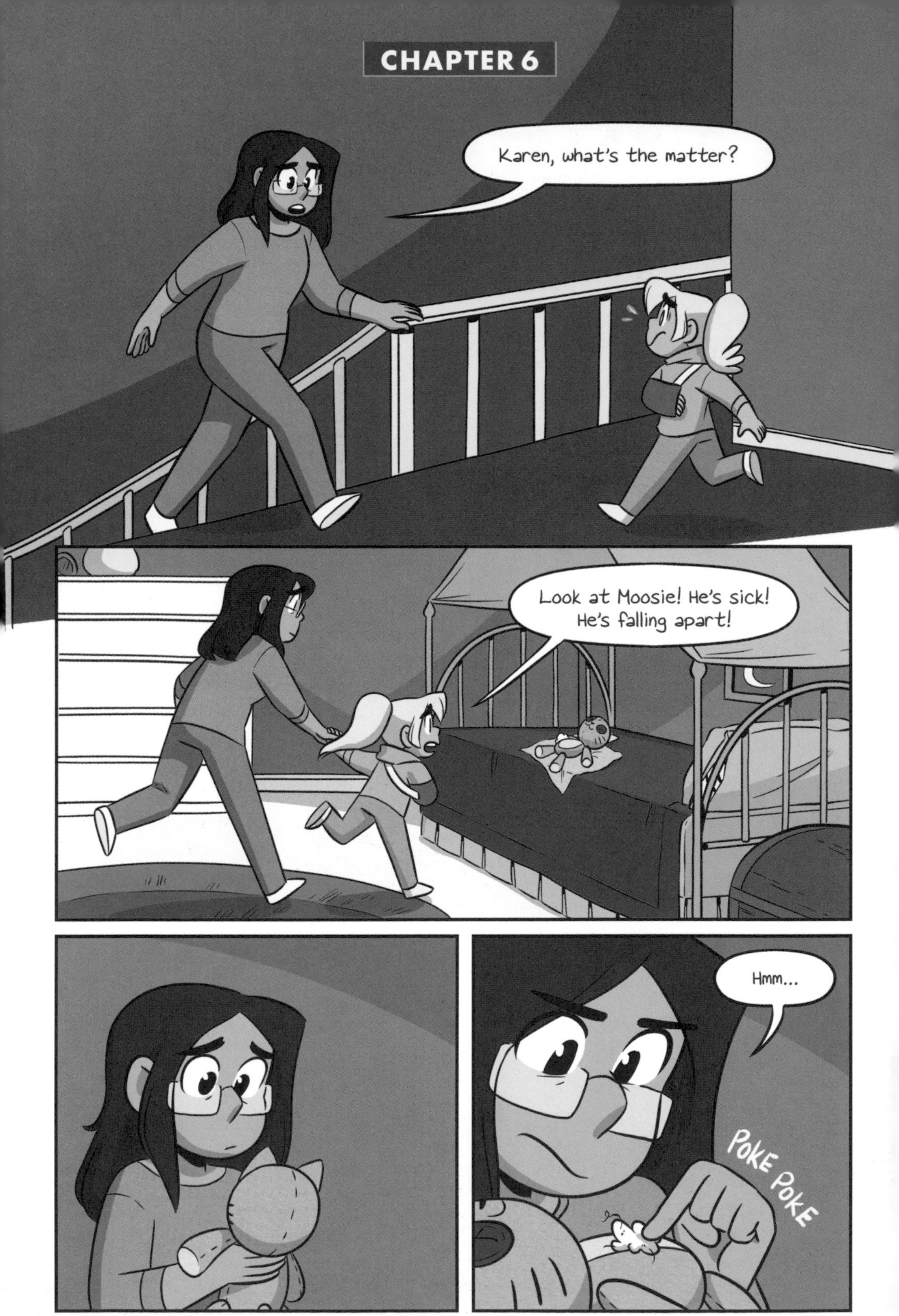
Karen, what's the matter?
Look at Moosie! He's sick! He's falling apart!
Hmm...
POKE POKE

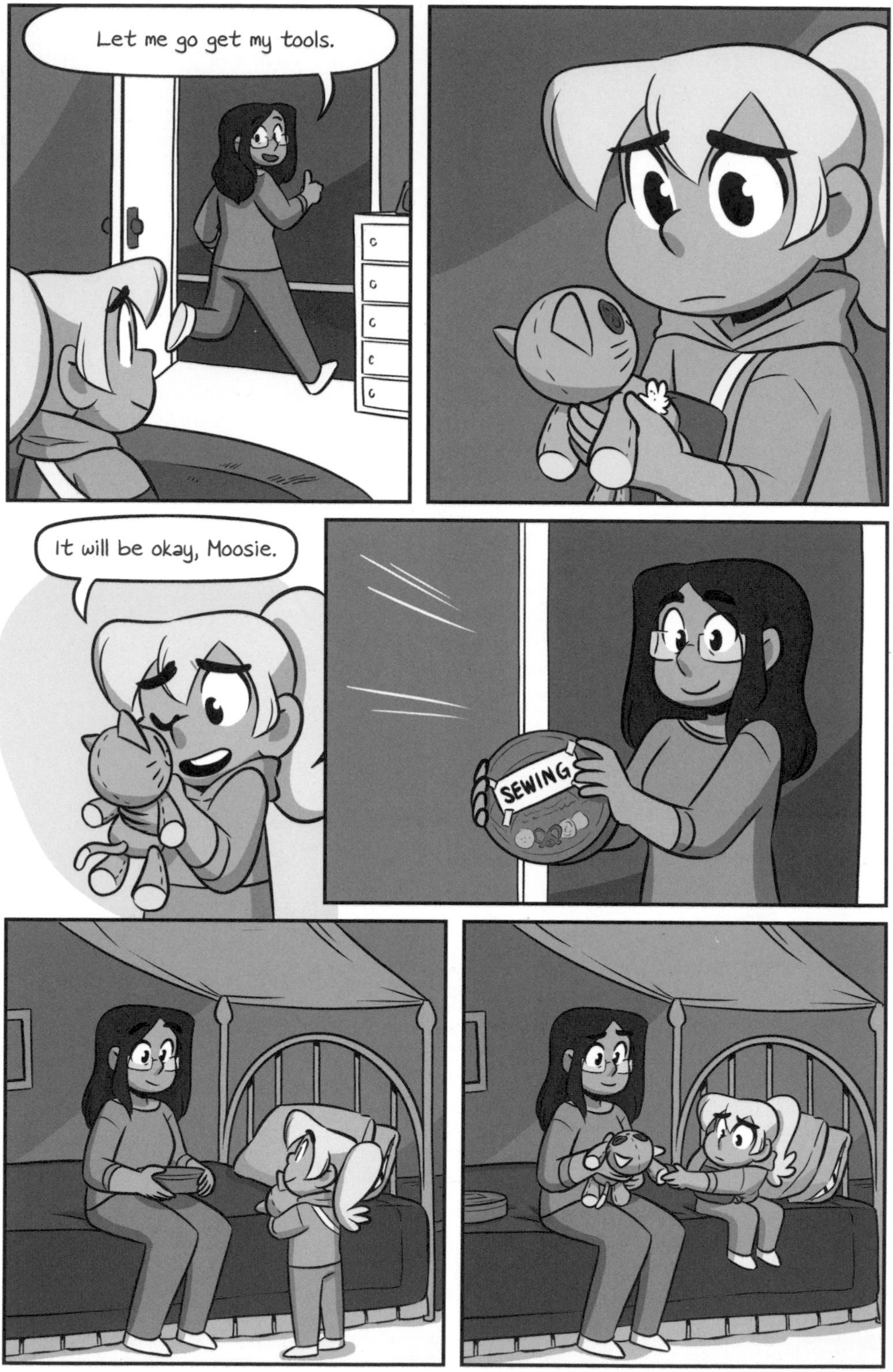
Let me go get my tools.
It will be okay, Moosie.
SEWING

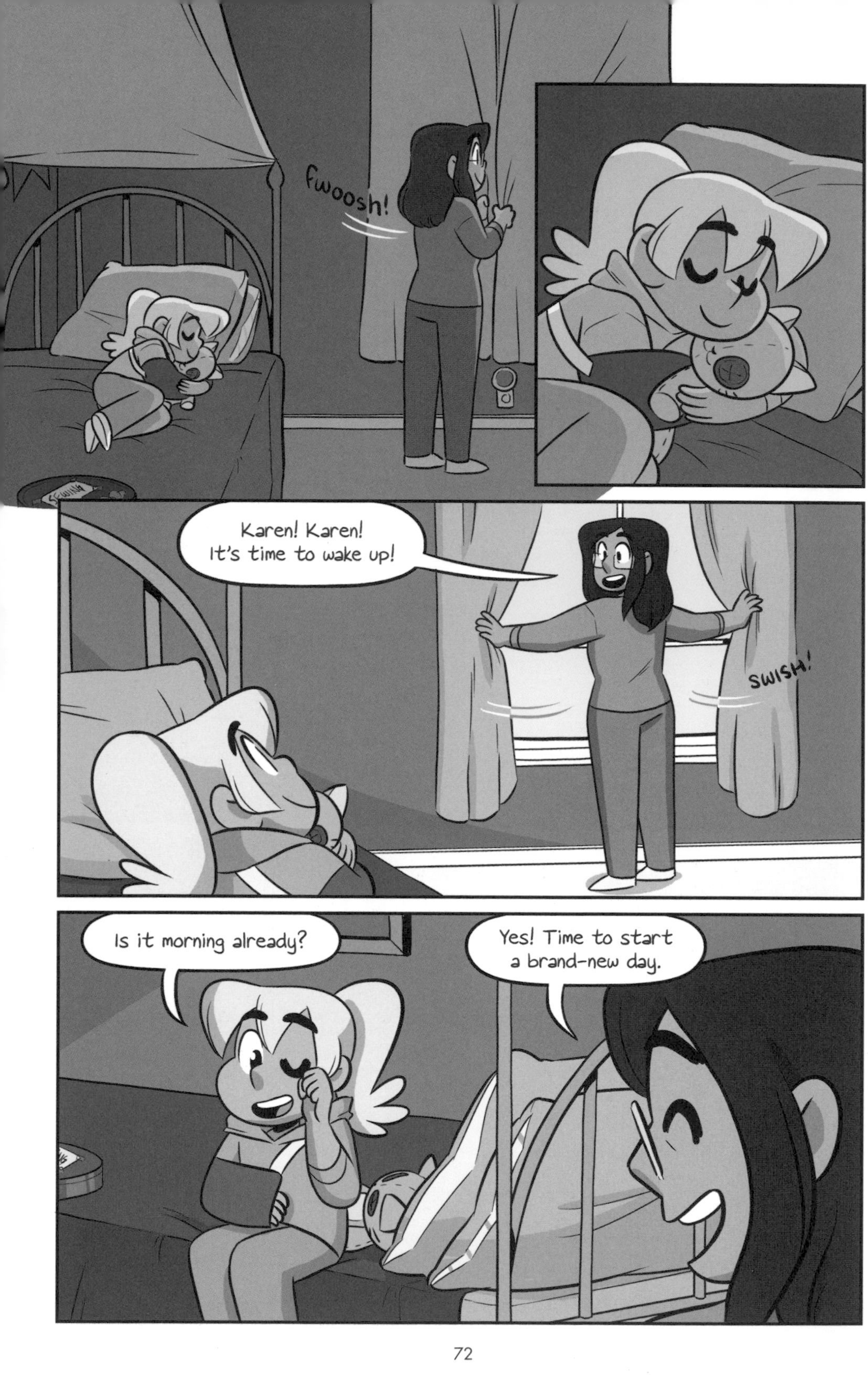
fwoosh!
Karen! Karen! It's time to wake up!
SWISH!
Is it morning already?
Yes! Time to start a brand-new day.

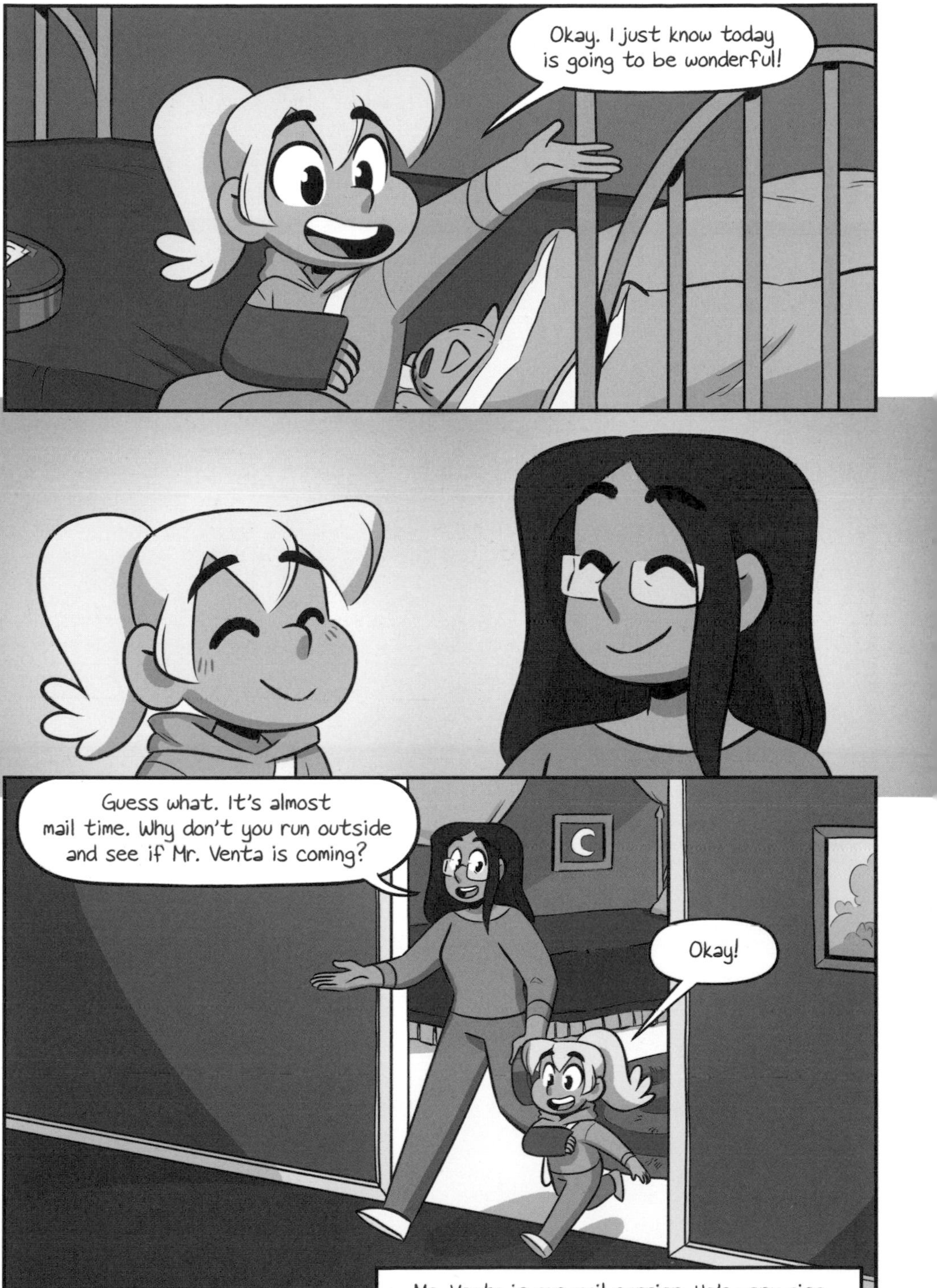
Okay. I just know today is going to be wonderful!
Guess what. It's almost mail time. Why don't you run outside and see if Mr. Venta is coming?
Okay!
Mr. Venta is our mail carrier. He's very nice and always hands me all the mail for the house.

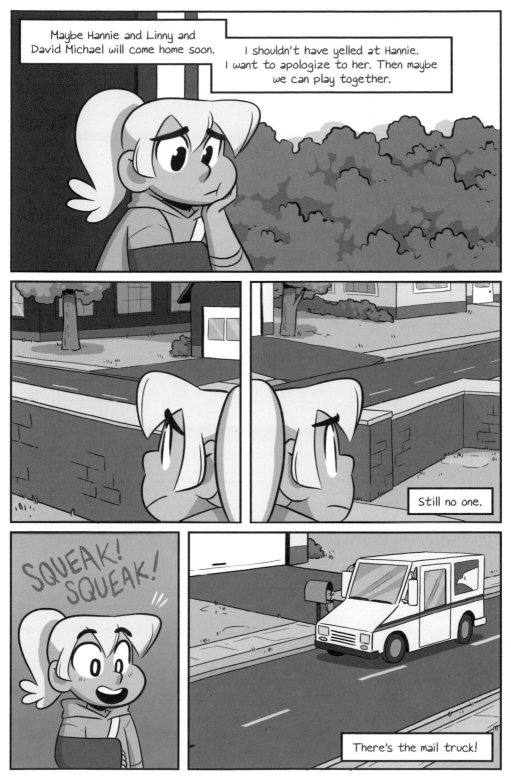

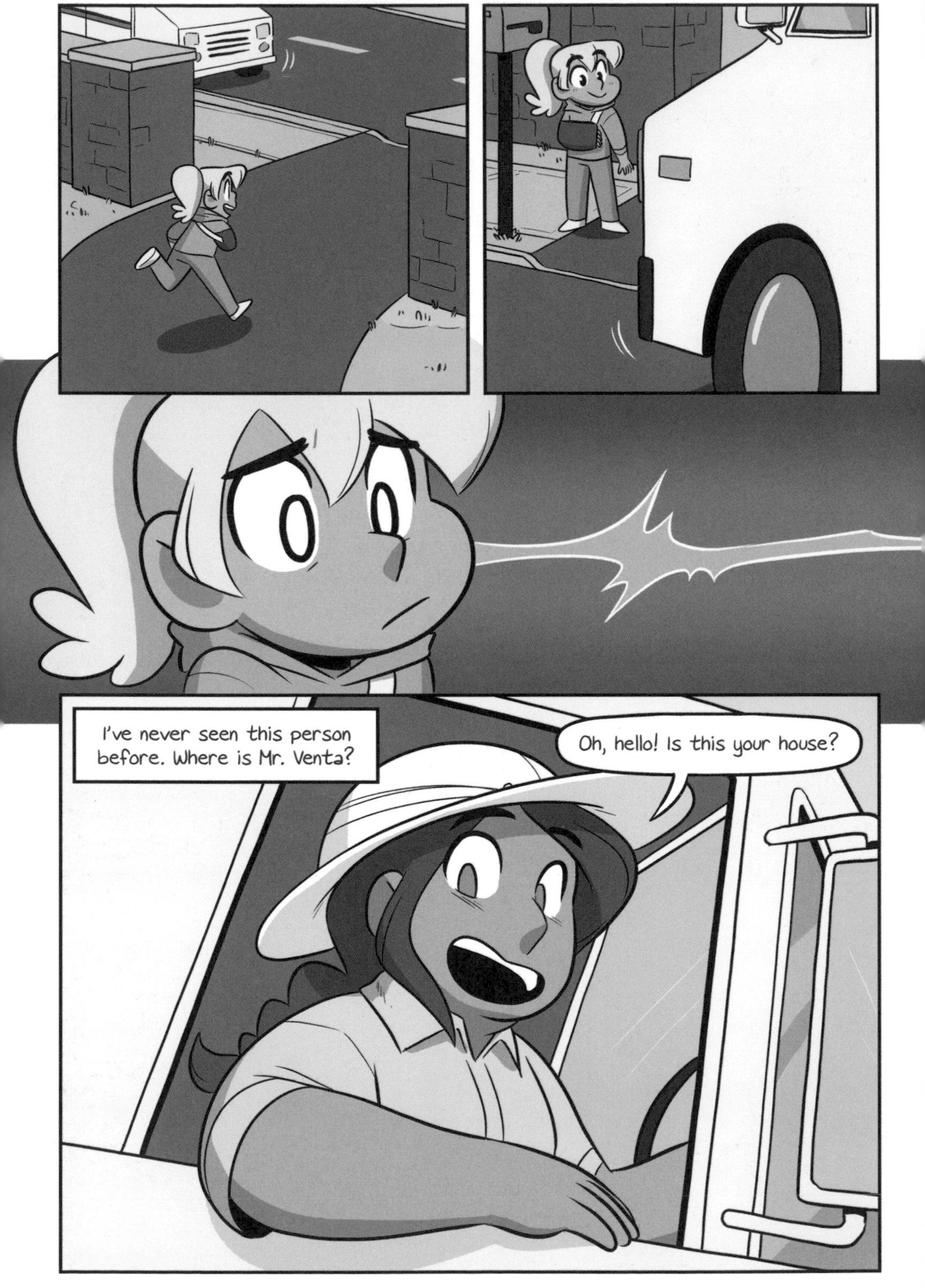
I've never seen this person before. Where is Mr. Venta?
Oh, hello! Is this your house?

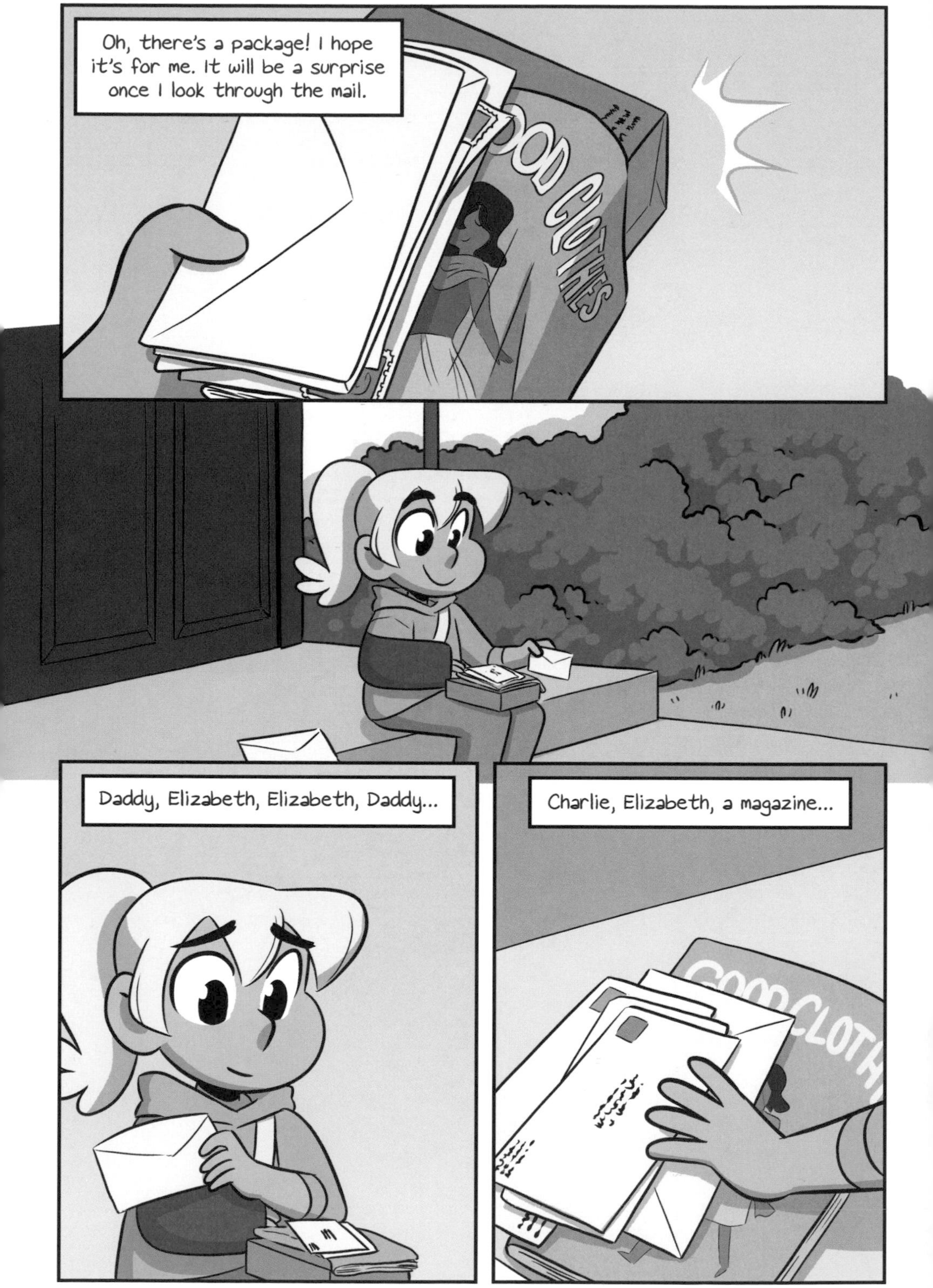
Oh, there's a package! I hope it's for me. It will be a surprise once I look through the mail.
GOOD CLOTHES
Daddy, Elizabeth, Elizabeth, Daddy...
Charlie, Elizabeth, a magazine...

CHAPTER 7

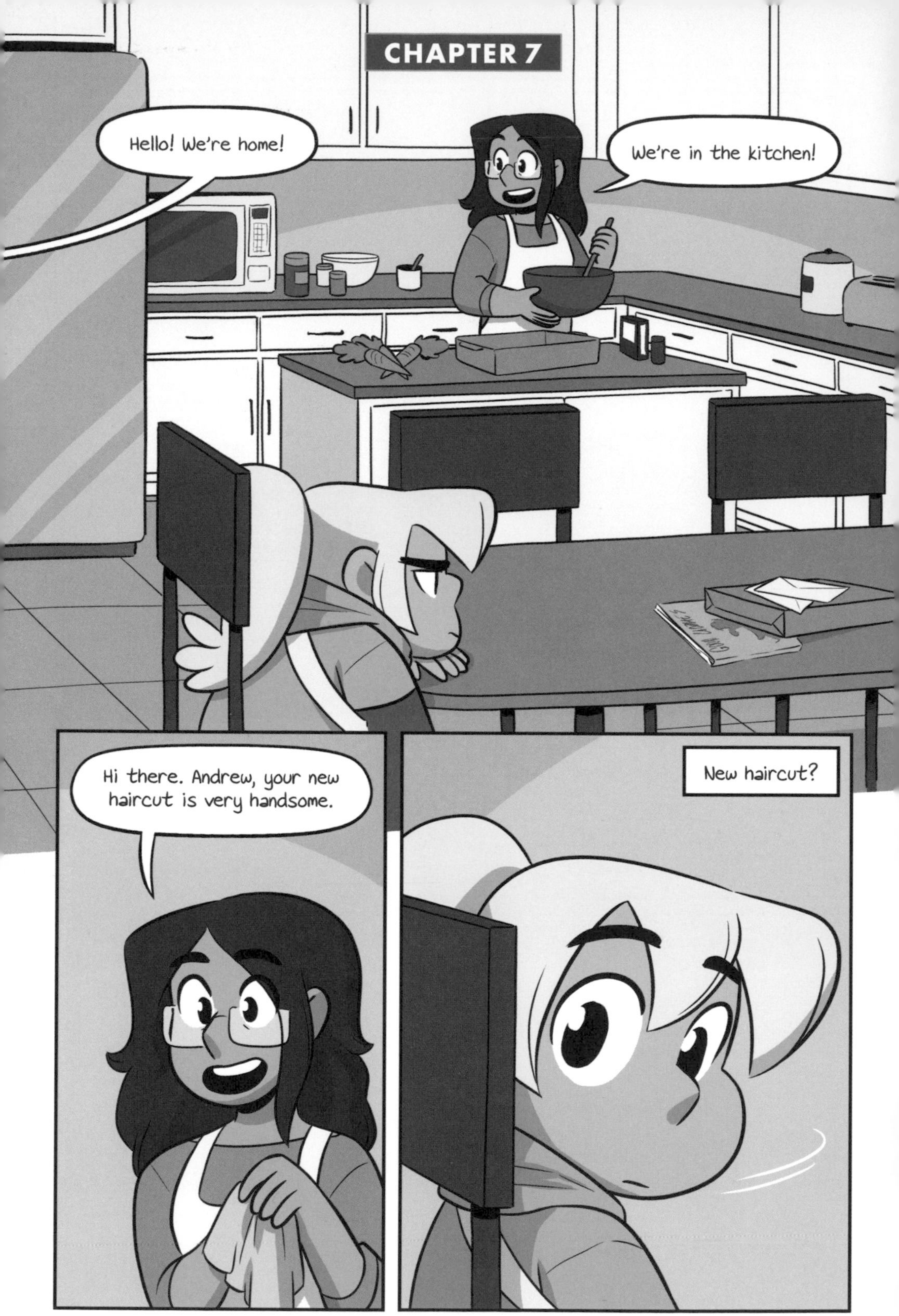
Hello! We're home!
We're in the kitchen!
Hi there. Andrew, your new haircut is very handsome.
New haircut?

88

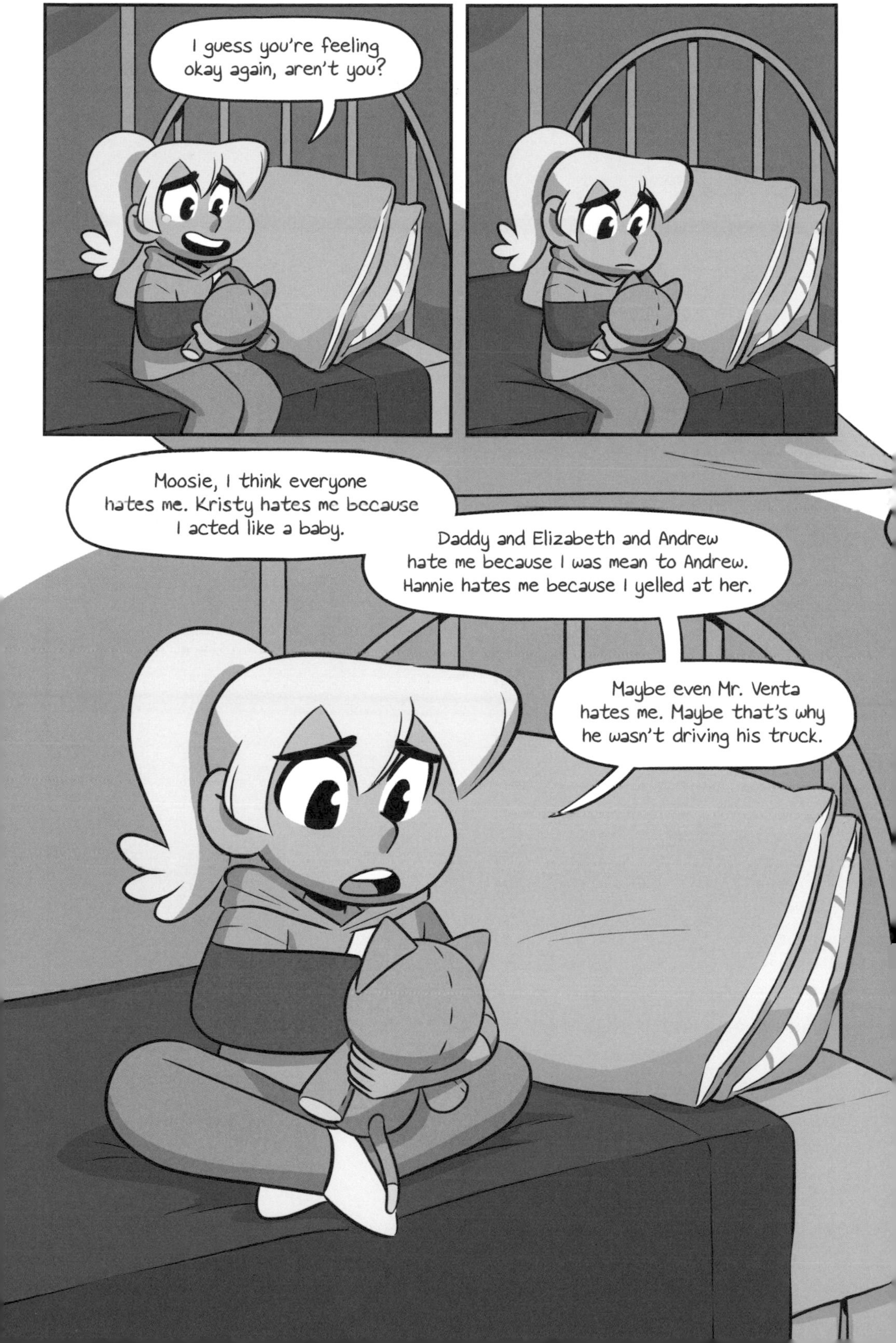
I guess you're feeling okay again, aren't you?
Moosie, I think everyone hates me. Kristy hates me because I acted like a baby.
Daddy and Elizabeth and Andrew hate me because I was mean to Andrew. Hannie hates me because I yelled at her.
Maybe even Mr. Venta hates me. Maybe that's why he wasn't driving his truck.

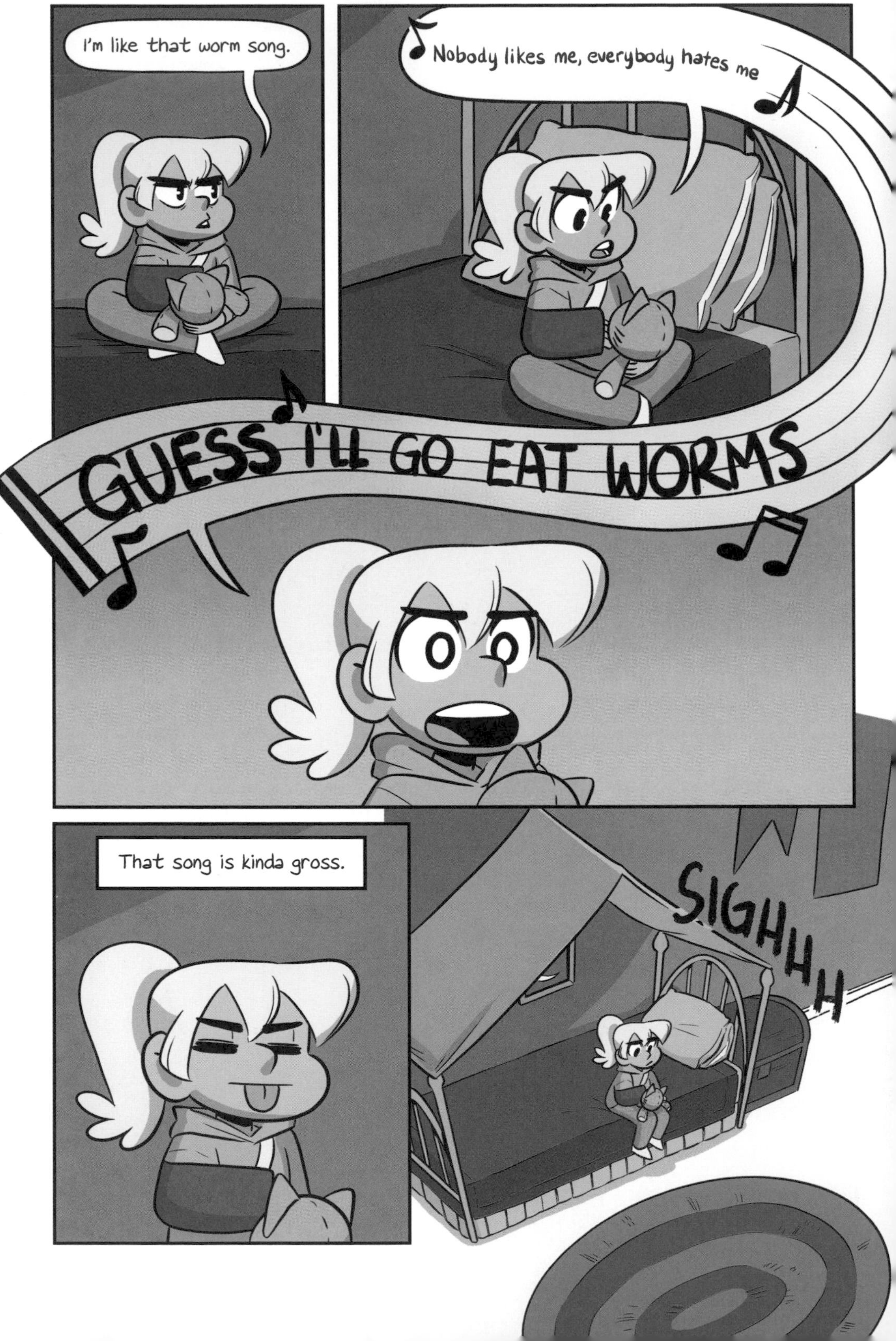
I'm like that worm song.
Nobody likes me, everybody hates me
GUESS I'LL GO EAT WORMS
That song is kinda gross.
SIGHHH

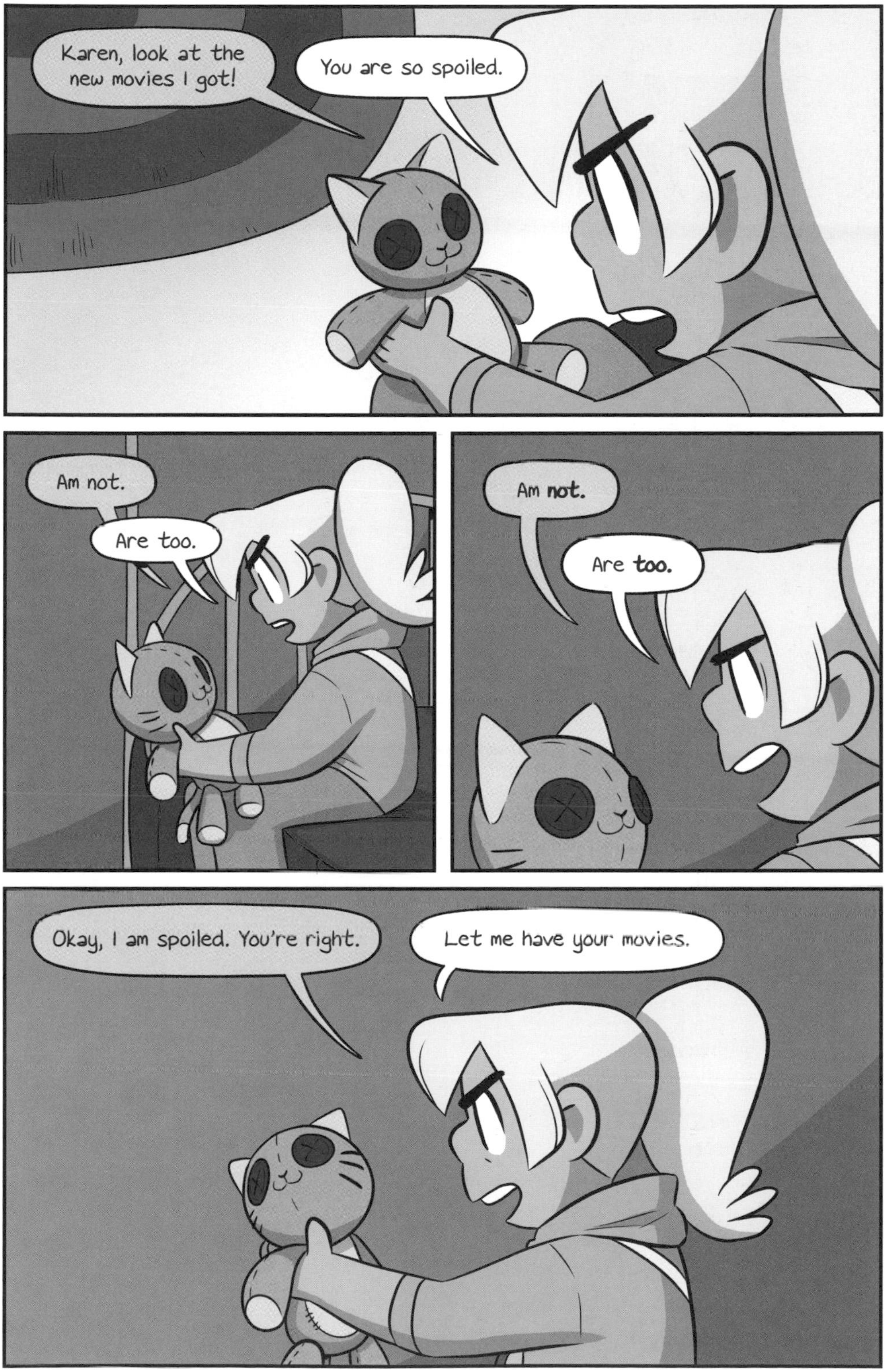
Karen, look at the new movies I got!
You are so spoiled.
Am not.
Are too.
Am **not.**
Are **too.**
Okay, I am spoiled. You're right.
Let me have your movies.

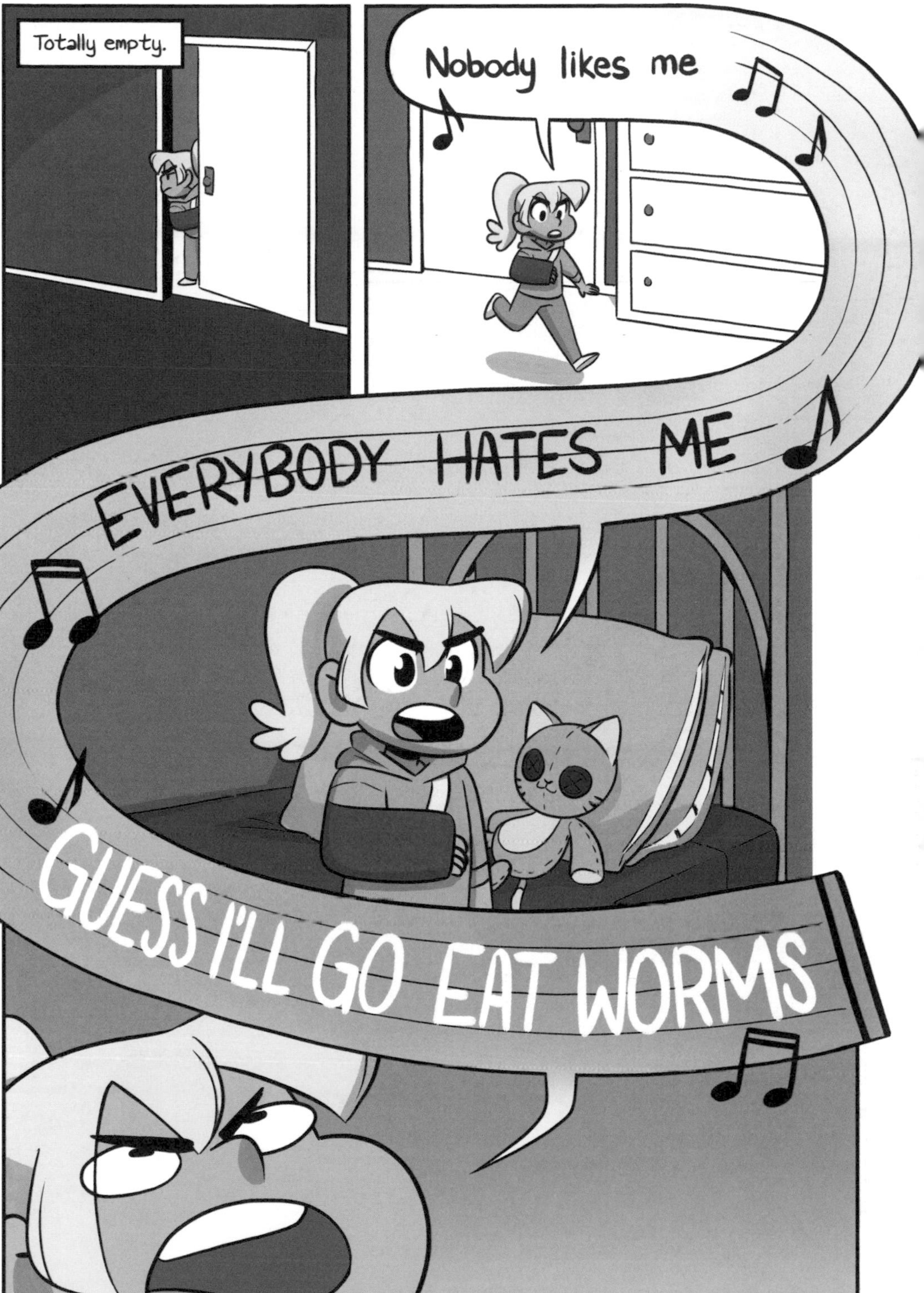
Totally empty.
Nobody likes me
EVERYBODY HATES ME
GUESS I'LL GO EAT WORMS

CHAPTER 8

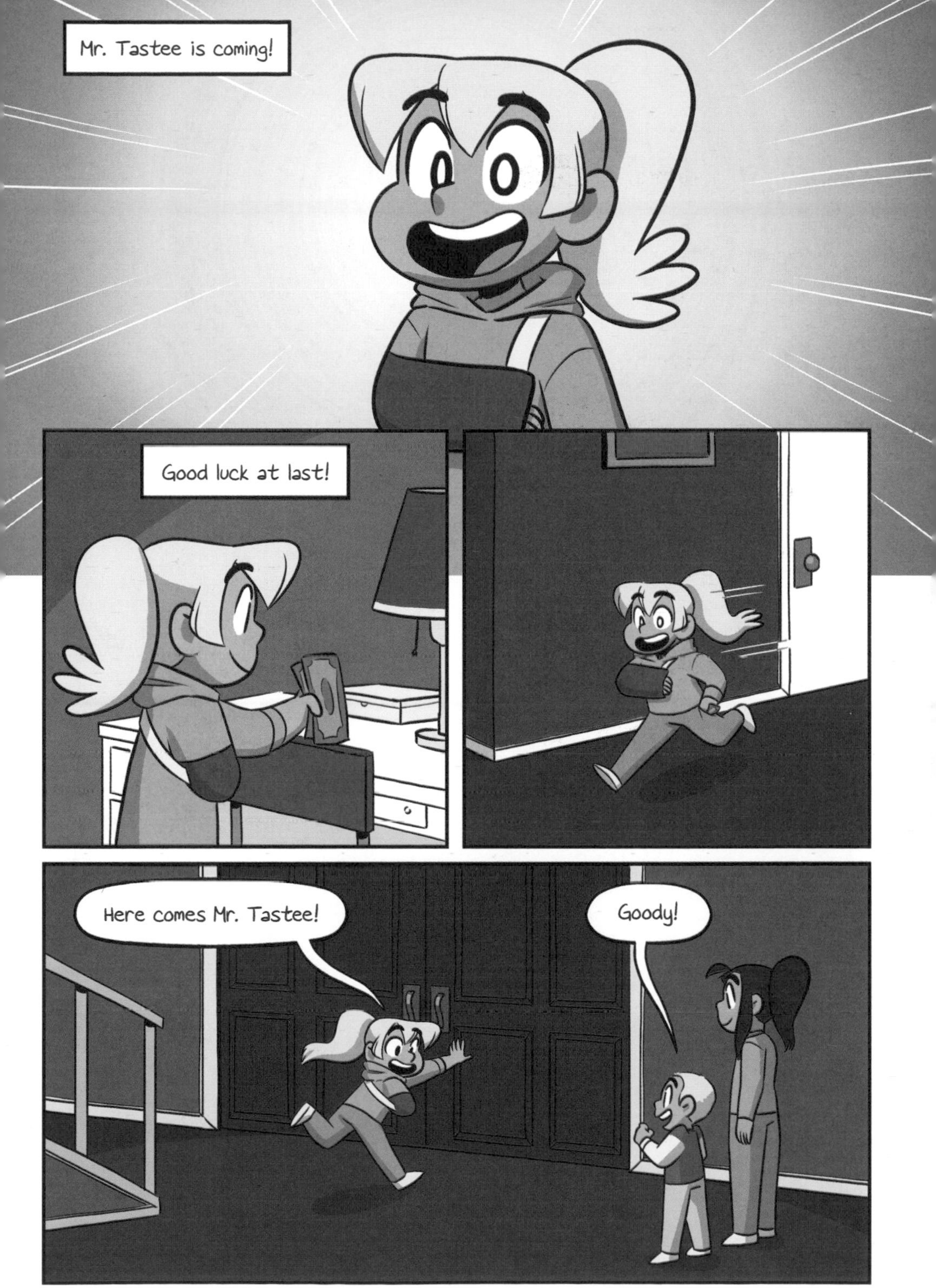
Mr. Tastee is coming!
Good luck at last!
Here comes Mr. Tastee!
Goody!

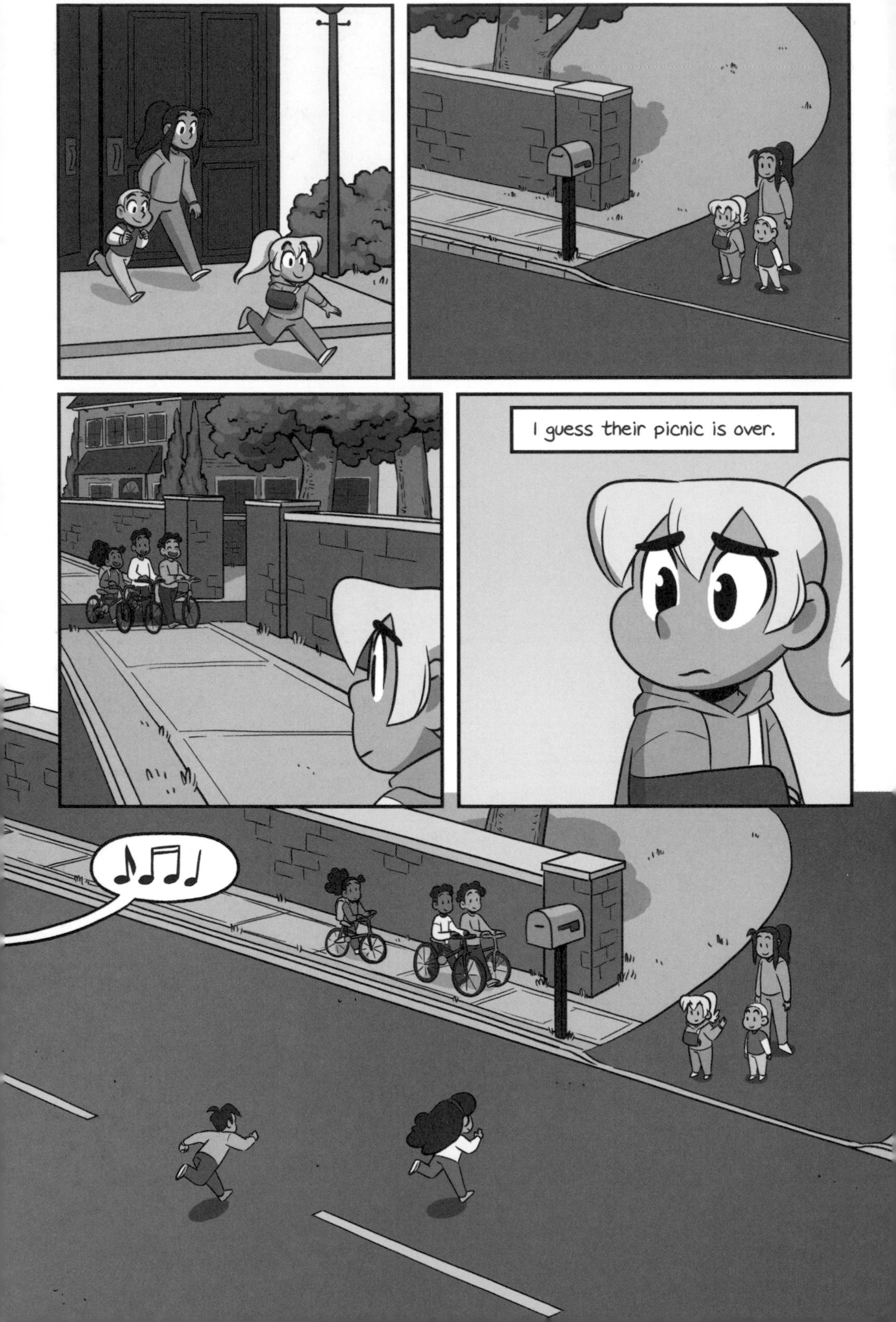
I guess their picnic is over.

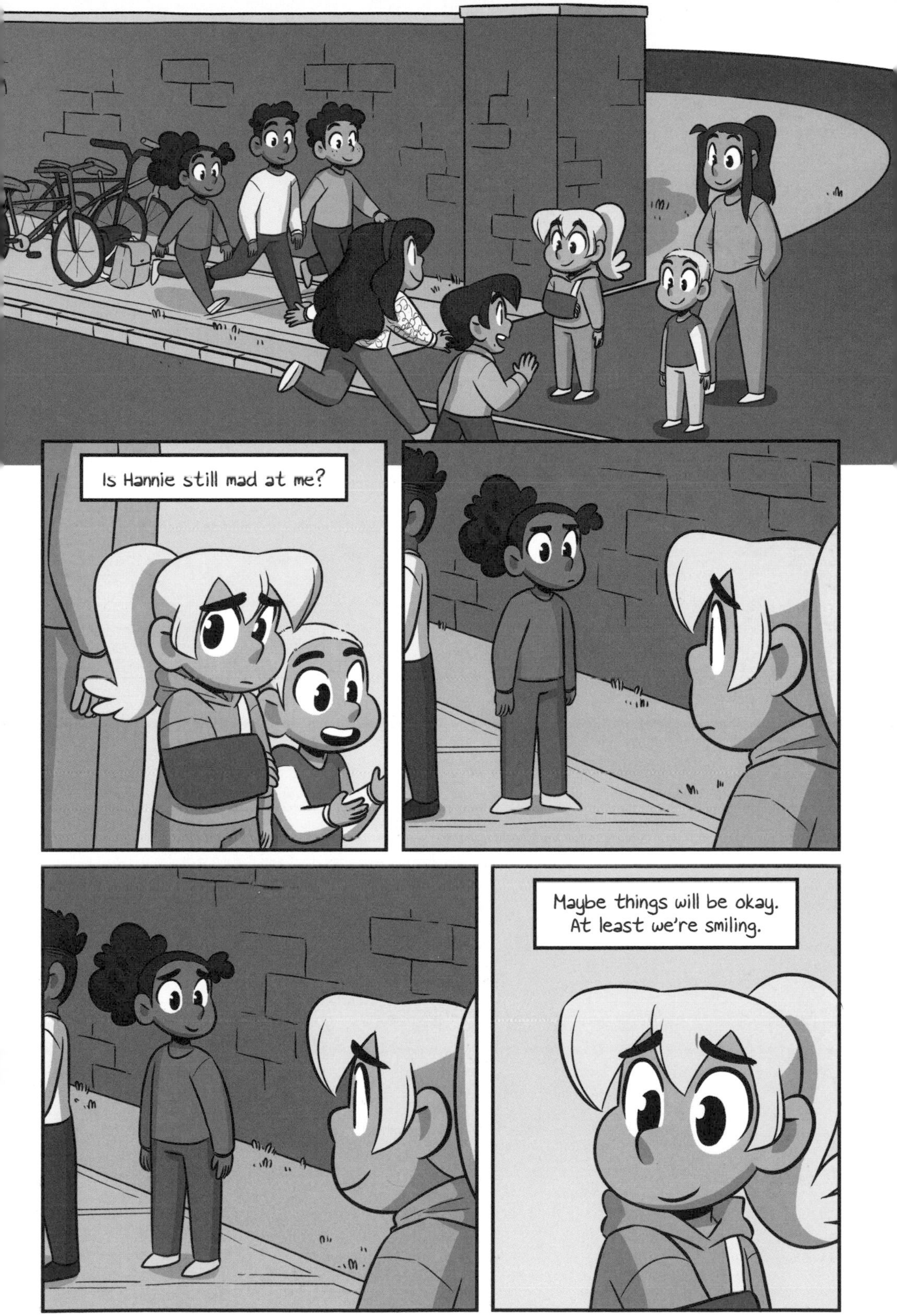
Is Hannie still mad at me?
Maybe things will be okay. At least we're smiling.

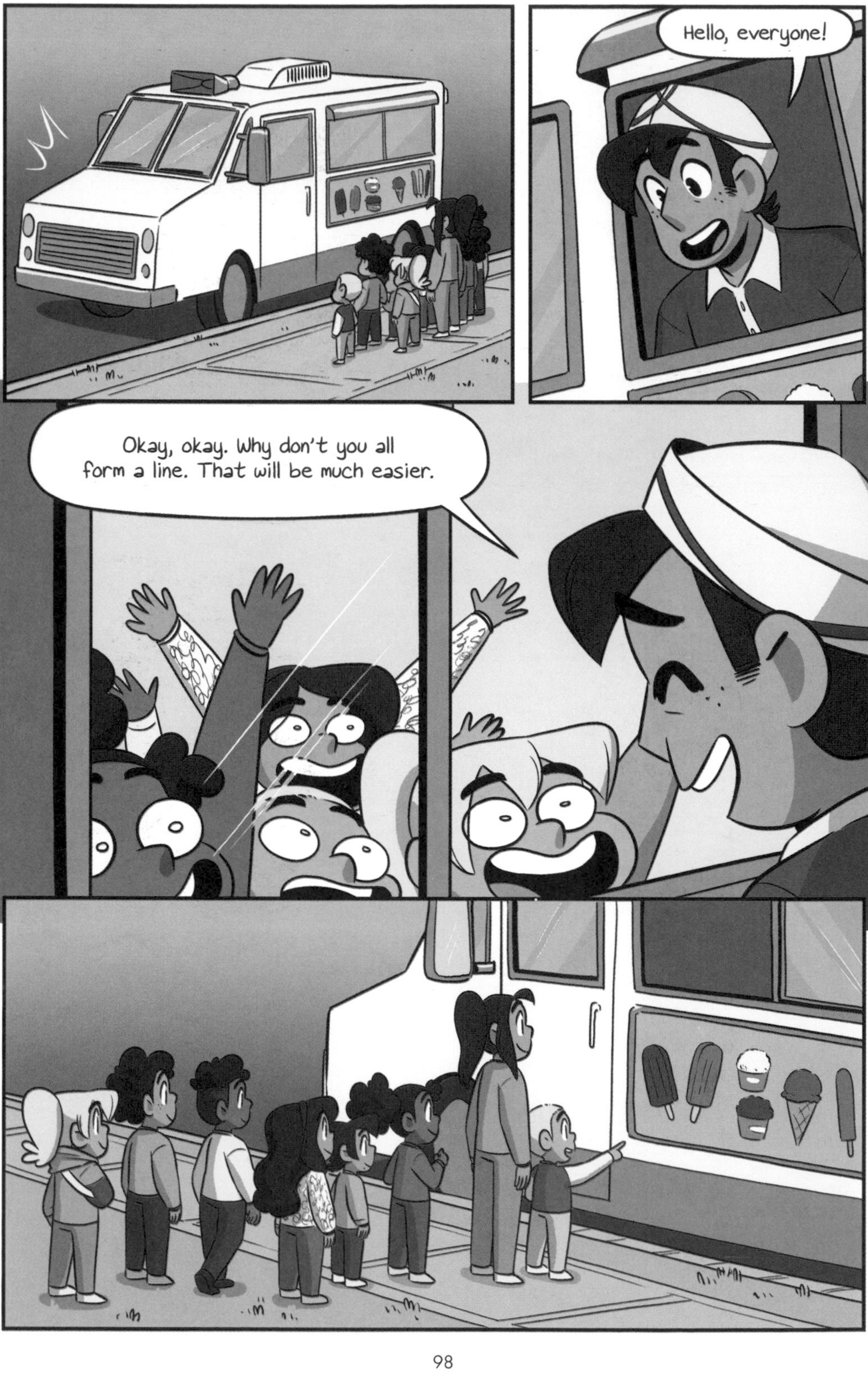
Hello, everyone!
Okay, okay. Why don't you all form a line. That will be much easier.

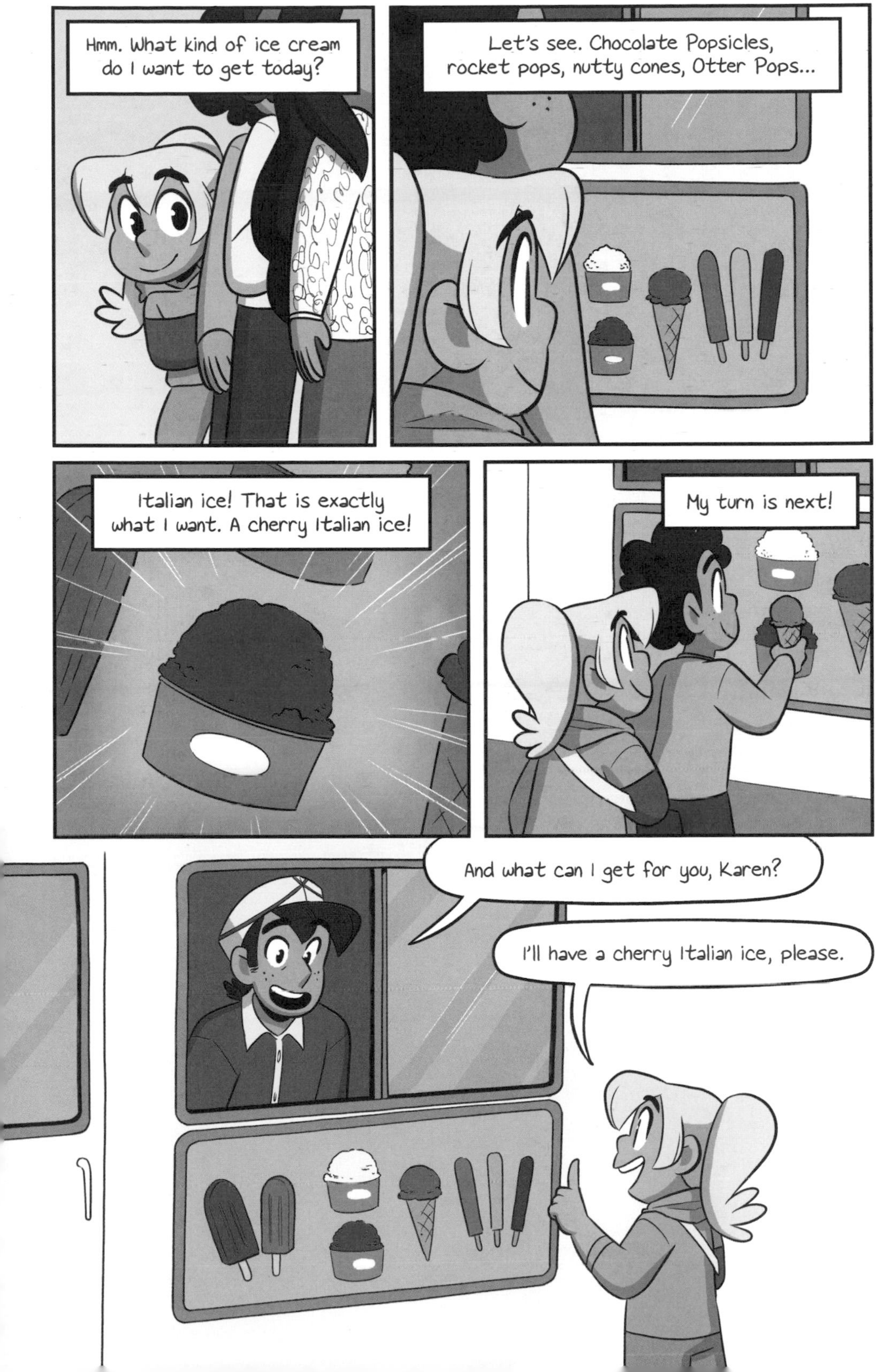
Hmm. What kind of ice cream do I want to get today?
Let's see. Chocolate Popsicles, rocket pops, nutty cones, Otter Pops...
Italian ice! That is exactly what I want. A cherry Italian ice!
My turn is next!
And what can I get for you, Karen?
I'll have a cherry Italian ice, please.

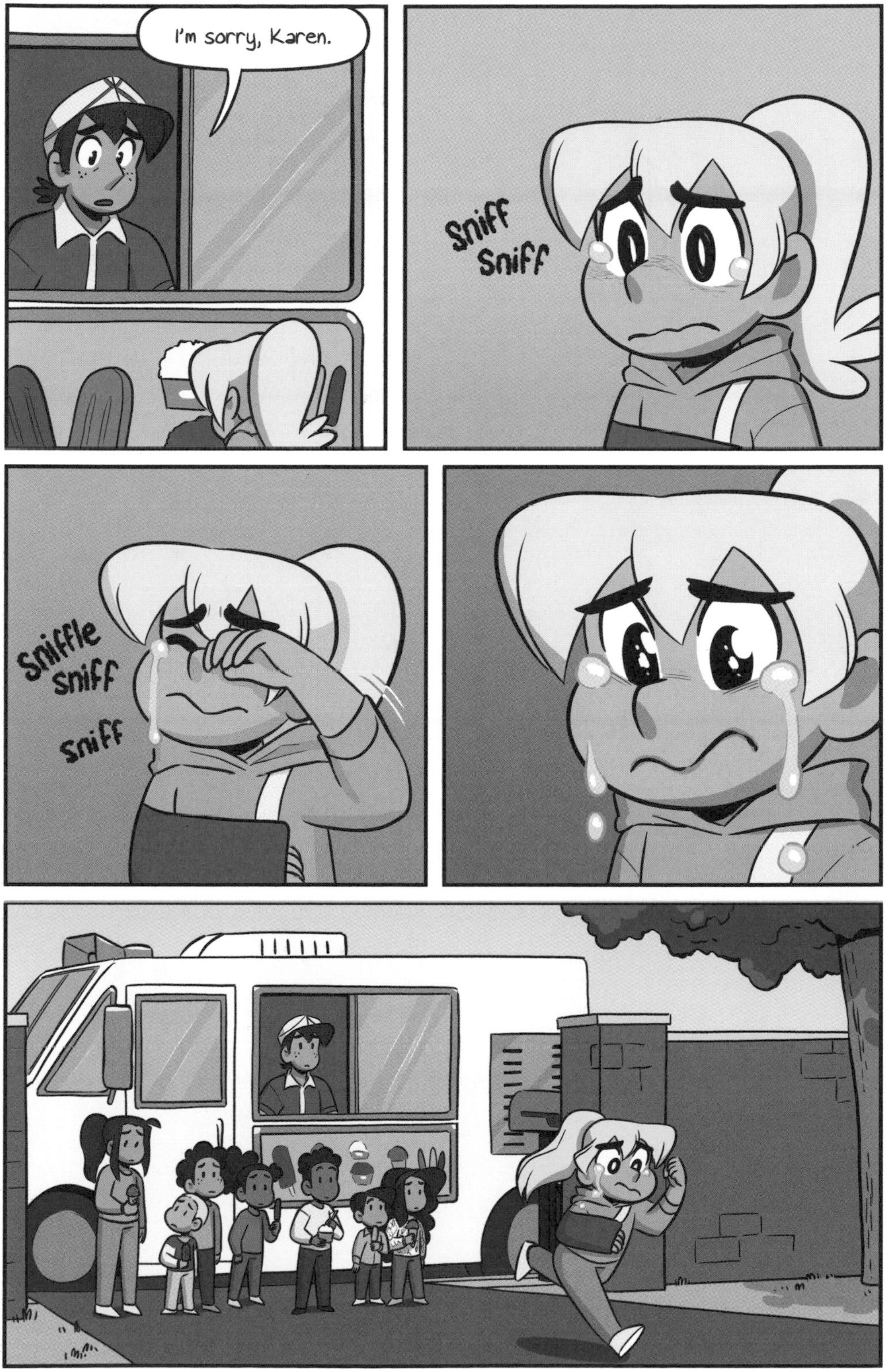
I'm sorry, Karen.
Sniff
Sniff
Sniffle
sniff
sniff

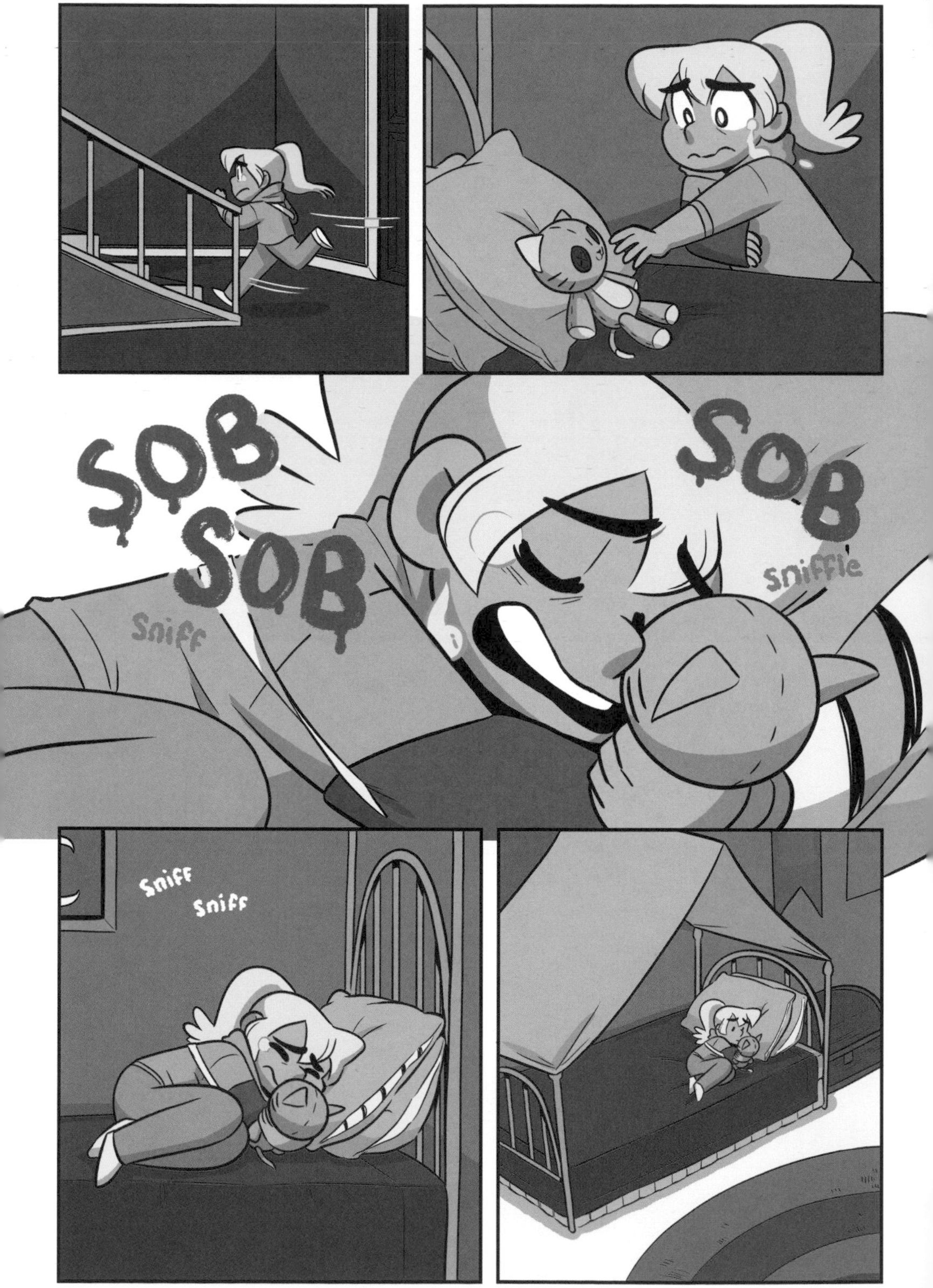
SOB
SOB
Sniff
SOB
sniffle
Sniff
Sniff

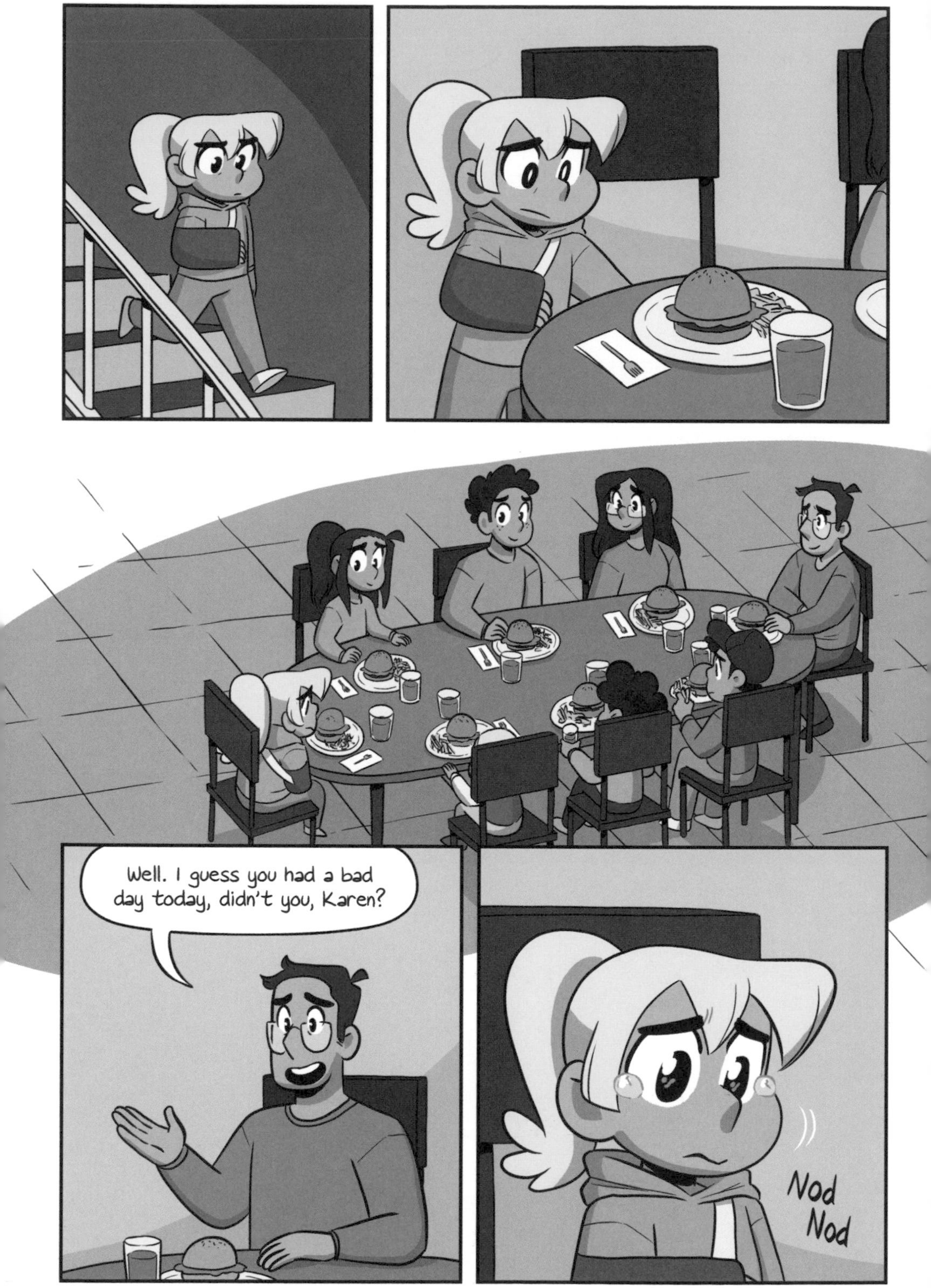
Well. I guess you had a bad day today, didn't you, Karen?
Nod Nod

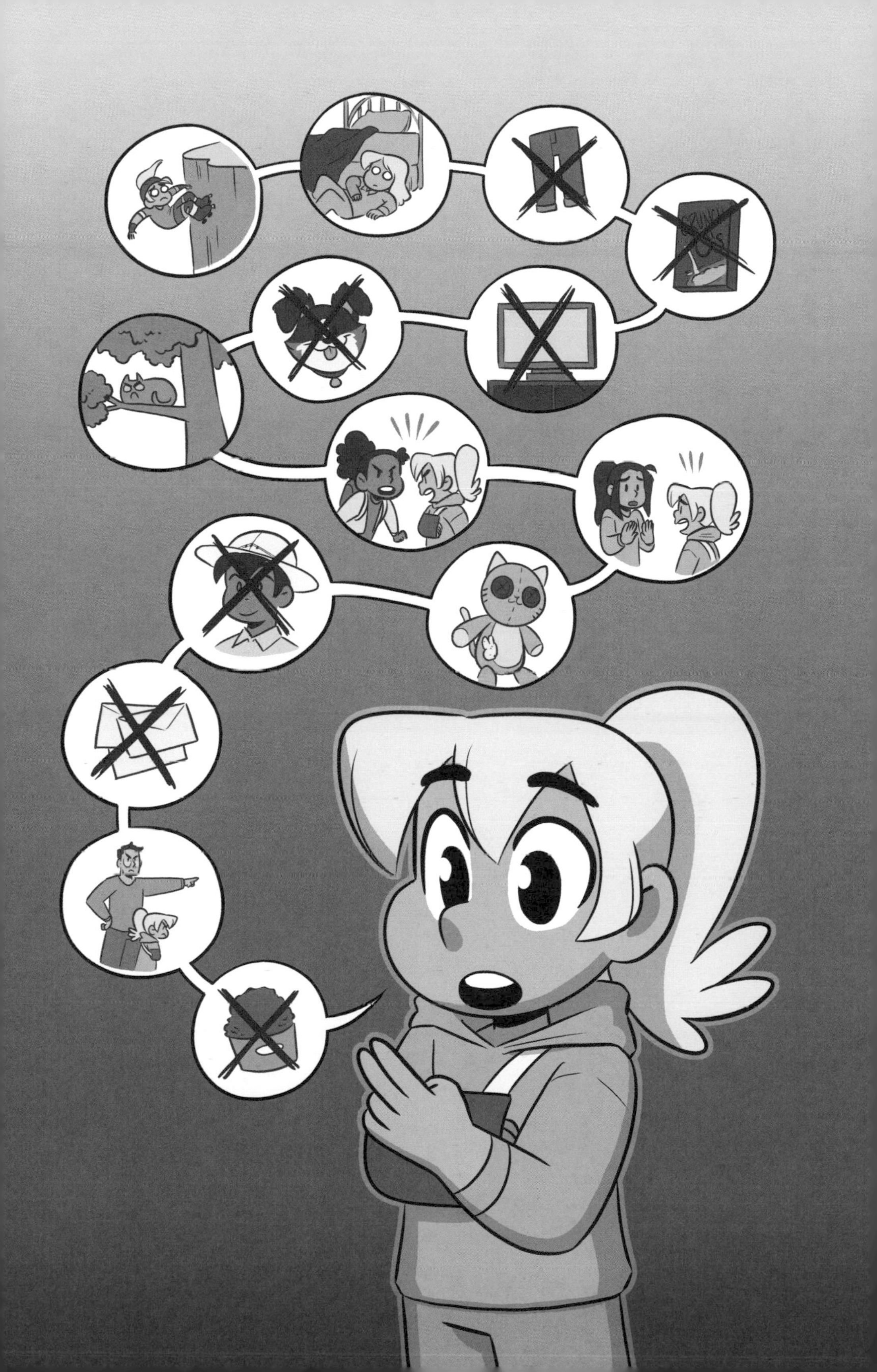

CHAPTER 9

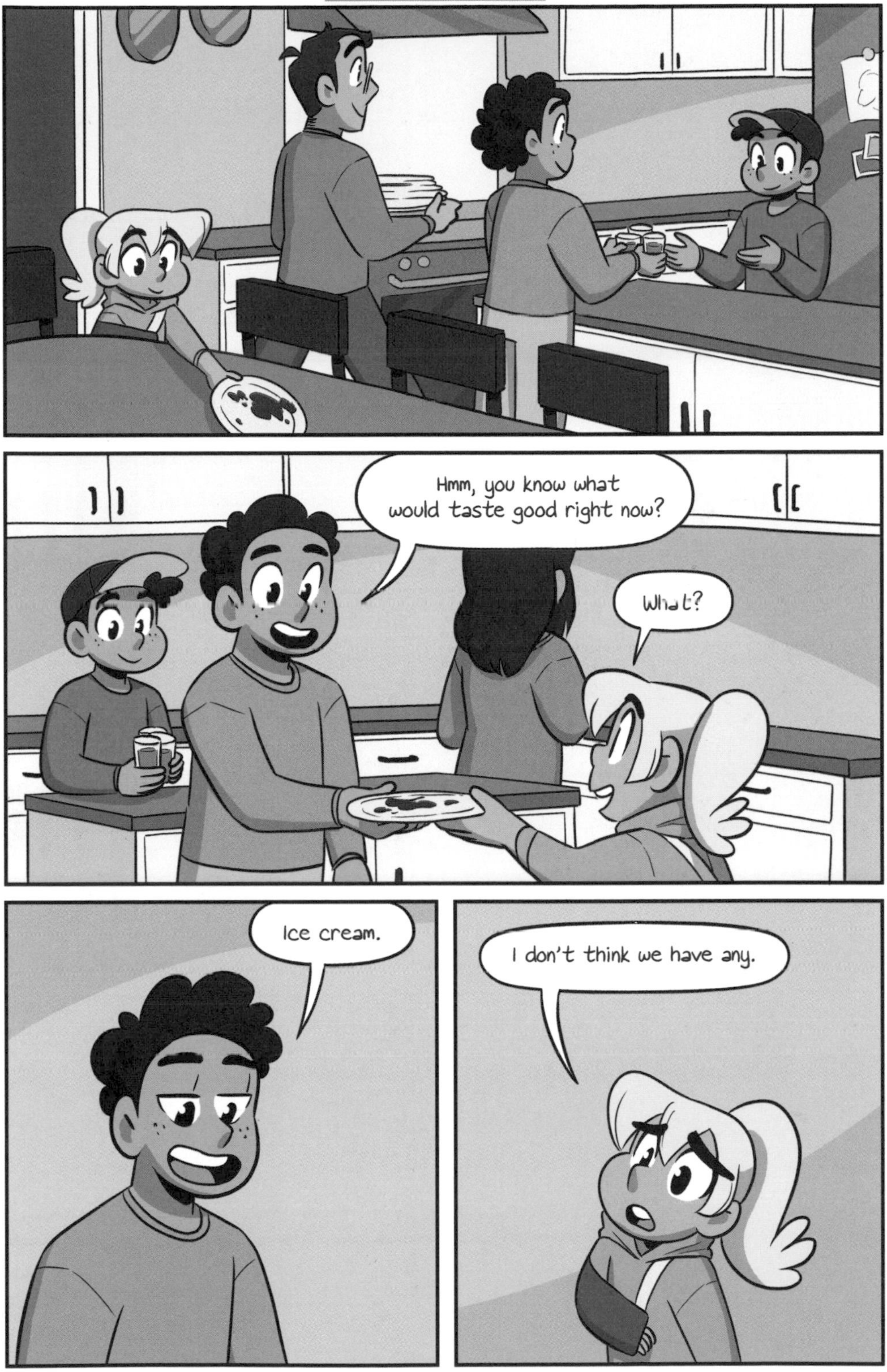
Hmm, you know what would taste good right now?
What?
Ice cream.
I don't think we have any.

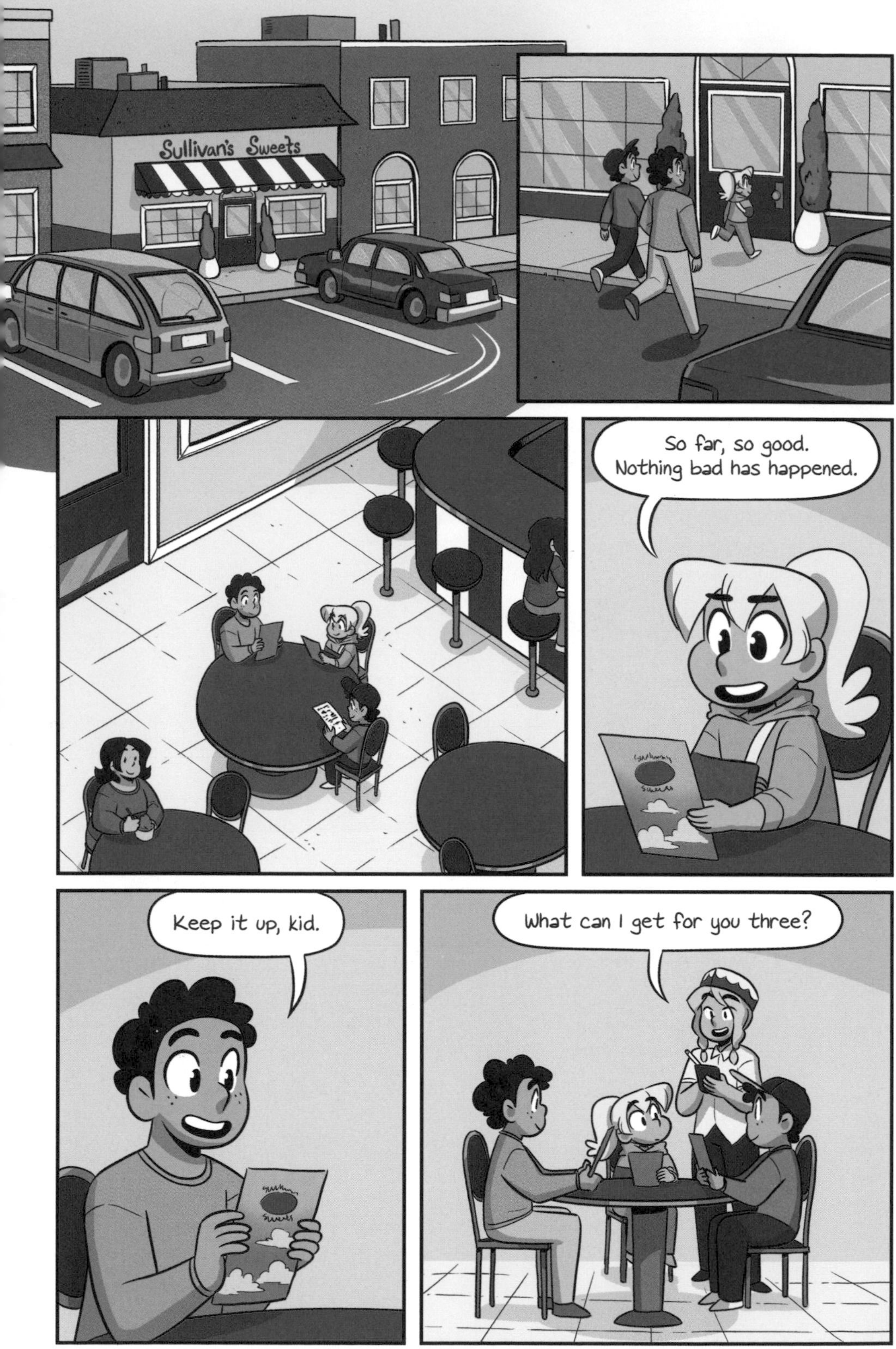
Sullivan's Sweets
So far, so good. Nothing bad has happened.
Keep it up, kid.
What can I get for you three?

116

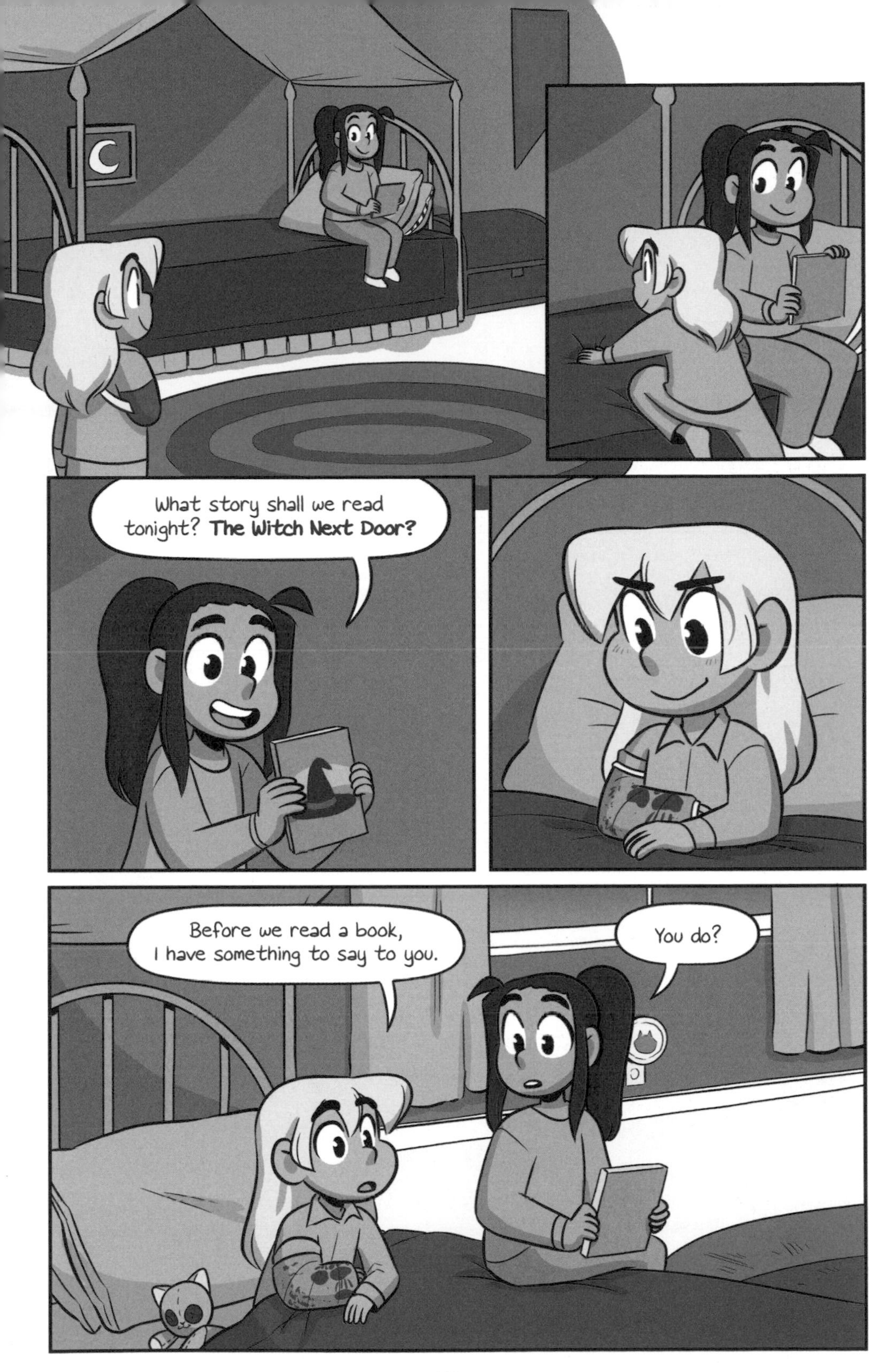
What story shall we read tonight? **The Witch Next Door?**
Before we read a book, I have something to say to you.
You do?

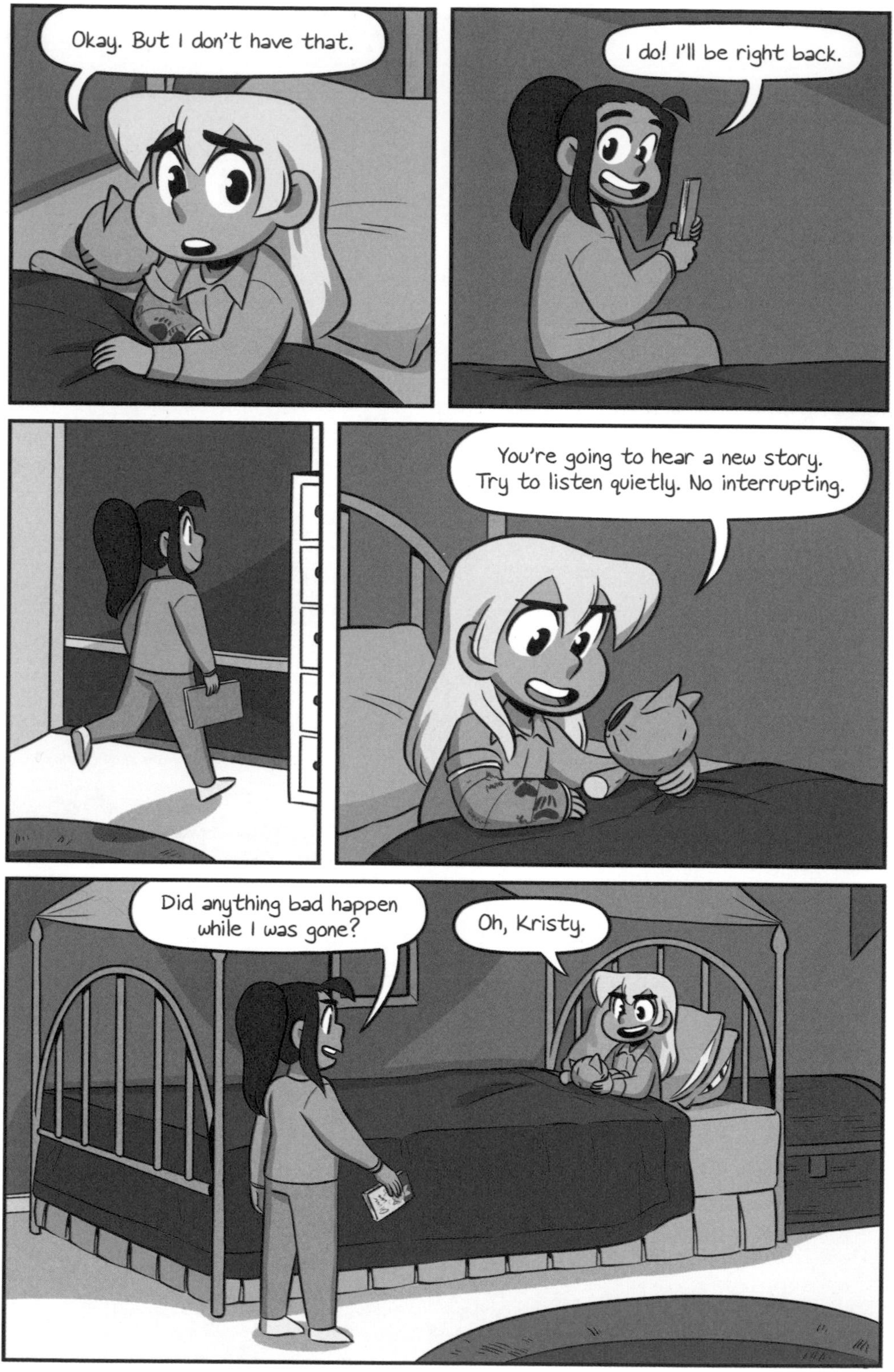
Okay. But I don't have that.
I do! I'll be right back.
You're going to hear a new story. Try to listen quietly. No interrupting.
Did anything bad happen while I was gone?
Oh, Kristy.

ANN M. MARTIN'S The Baby-sitters Club is one of the most popular series in the history of publishing — with more than 180 million books in print worldwide — and inspired a generation of young readers. Her novels include *Belle Teal, A Corner of the Universe* (a Newbery Honor book), *Here Today, A Dog's Life,* and *On Christmas Eve,* as well as the much-loved collaborations, *P.S. Longer Letter Later* and *Snail Mail No More,* with Paula Danziger, and *The Doll People* and *The Meanest Doll in the World,* written with Laura Godwin and illustrated by Brian Selznick. She lives in upstate New York.

KATY FARINA is the creator of the *New York Times* bestselling graphic novel adaptations of *Karen's Witch* and *Karen's Roller Skates* by Ann M. Martin. She has painted backgrounds for *She-Ra and the Princesses of Power* at DreamWorks TV and has also done work for BOOM! Studios, Oni Press, and Z2 Comics. She lives in Los Angeles. Visit her online at katyfarina.com.

DON'T MISS THE OTHER BABY-SITTERS LITTLE SISTER GRAPHIC NOVELS!

A GRAPHIC NOVEL BY
KATY FARINA
BABY-SITTERS LITTLE SISTER
KAREN'S WITCH
BASED ON THE NOVEL BY
ANN M. MARTIN

A GRAPHIC NOVEL BY
KATY FARINA
BABY-SITTERS LITTLE SISTER
KAREN'S ROLLER SKATES
BASED ON THE NOVEL BY
ANN M. MARTIN

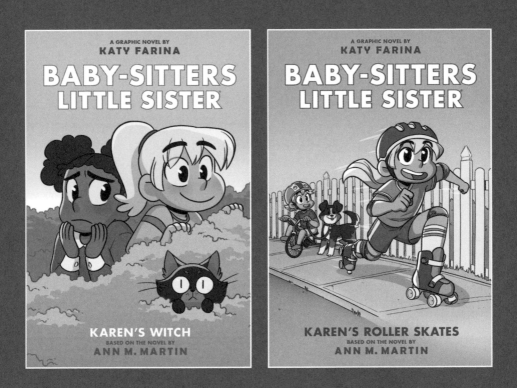